MOLTEN HEART

BBC

DOCTOR WHO

MOLTEN HEART

UNA MCCORMACK

BOOKS

1 3 5 7 9 10 8 6 4 2

BBC Books, an imprint of Ebury Publishing
20 Vauxhall Bridge Road,
London SW1V 2SA

BBC Books is part of the Penguin Random House group of companies whose
addresses can be found at global.penguinrandomhouse.com

Penguin
Random House
UK

Doctor Who is a BBC Wales production.
Executive producer: Chris Chibnall, Matt Strevens and Sam Hoyle

First published by BBC Books in 2018

www.penguin.co.uk

A CIP catalogue record for this book is available from the British Library

ISBN 978 1 785 94363 8

Publishing Director: Albert DePetrillo
Project Editor: Steve Cole
Cover Design: Lee Binding/Tealady Design
Production: Sian Pratley

Typeset in 11/14.3 pt Albertina MT Std
by Integra Software Services Pvt. Ltd, Pondicherry

Printed and bound in Great Britain by Clays Ltd, Elcograf S.p.A.

Penguin Random House is committed to a sustainable future for
our business, our readers and our planet. This book is made
from Forest Stewardship Council® certified paper.

MIX
Paper from
responsible sources
FSC® C018179
www.fsc.org

One

On the surface, this world seemed nothing special. One more rock, pocked and pitted, spinning slowly through the void of space. Empty.

The earliest voyagers to this part of space took one look at this world and passed by. Nothing to see here, they thought. Move along. Plenty more planets out there. A few hardier adventurers, or completists, took the time to land. They took a quick look around, satisfied their wanderlust or their need for a tick in a box, and then went on their way. When it came down to it, there really wasn't much to see. No curiously formed cities, no striking land formations or scarlet oceans, no indigenous sentient life, it seemed. The moors were nice enough (if you liked that sort of thing), and even the hardest of heart would have to admit that the flowers were pretty (who doesn't like that sort of thing?), and the seas held quite a few fish and made some pleasant beaches, some sandy, some with charming pebbles (if you collected that kind of thing) – but the truth was you could see everything like this somewhere else, and you didn't have to travel anywhere near as far to see it.

People came and said, "Oh, that's nice," and then left and more or less forgot they'd ever been there. Every now and then an empire would come past and claim the planet for its own: someone would nip down to the surface and plant a flag, or maybe even put a satellite in orbit. Sometimes someone else nipped down and planted a different kind of flag a few miles away, just to make a point. The flags didn't last, not in the great scheme of things. The orbits of the satellites would decay, and the little machines would come crashing to the ground, making one more hole in the surface of this unobtrusive world. The empires would decay too, in time, and for a few thousand years or so the planet would be left to its own devices once again, patiently weathering the meteors and asteroids that occasionally dropped by, getting on quietly with its business.

No, on the surface there really wasn't much to see. Rocks. Grass. More rocks. Some water. Sand (or pebbles). Back to rocks and grass again. The average traveller would take one look and move along. Nothing to see.

So much for the average traveller. But the best travellers – the very best – aren't fooled by surfaces. The best travellers know that if they want to find treasures, they must dig, dig deep, below the surface, down to the heart. And below the surface this world – Adamantine – indeed has many treasures to show. Many treasures, and some terrors, and always, always adventure. The best travellers always find adventure.

And the very best travellers in the whole of time and space are heading this way.

*

It hadn't taken Yaz long to notice that it was never completely quiet on the TARDIS. No, it was never that, not even when nobody was dashing around being excited. Even at the quietest moments, there was always a faint hum, reminding you that the ship was alive, sort of (she certainly wouldn't chance saying it *wasn't* alive, and certainly not when the TARDIS could hear) and that at any moment, something wonderful and marvellous and quite probably madly dangerous might suddenly start happening.

And Yaz loved it, loved every single second of it. The marvellous travelling, the wondrous marvels, and the marvellous wonders. And the danger: yes, she would have to admit that she liked that too. It was one of the reasons that she'd picked her career. Not because she thrived on danger, or got a kick from taking risks. Those people didn't get far. No, Yaz was the kind of person who stayed cool when other people panicked. That made her feel useful, helpful, and in control. Yaz knew that when things were going wrong, she was the kind of person who could make a difference. What her time on the TARDIS was teaching her was on what scale she could make that difference.

She spent her "off-duty" time, as she sometimes thought of it, wandering this amazing ship: exploring, checking for exits (Yaz was practical and sensible too), and trying to understand something of the nature of her new digs. Eventually, she would come back to the console room, and there, inevitably, she would find the Doctor, this most wonderful and marvellous of all the wonders and marvels that Yaz had recently seen; this incredible traveller and adventurer; source of fun; force for good; friend and mentor. Yaz had wondered a couple of times what she would do when her time with the Doctor was over. Would she be able to go back to her job, her old life? Would anything ever seem as brilliant and exciting again? She would put these thoughts aside. Time to worry later about the future. For now, enjoy the present – or whatever time it was when the TARDIS happened to land.

Coming into the console room, Yaz found the Doctor all by herself. She was unusually quiet too – for the Doctor – but still plainly busy. The Doctor was gripping the console with both hands, murmuring something... Coordinates? Some new language? A recipe? A spell? French verbs? You never quite knew. But there was always something. Yaz got the feeling that the Doctor didn't rest – not really – and that her mind was always ticking away, absorbing some new piece of information. Learning, discovering, connecting, *thinking*...

Yaz, watching her, thought, *I want to be like that...*

The Doctor saw her and smiled. "Hullo," she said. "Still looking round?"

"I was wondering about emergency exits," said Yaz. "You never know when you'll need them."

"Tell me about it," said the Doctor, and turned back to the console.

"Is it OK?" said Yaz. "Me looking round?"

The Doctor looked up and gave that wide, welcoming smile. "Of course! My place is your place, or whatever they say. Just, er, don't press every button you find." The Doctor thought about that. "Actually, don't press *any* button you find."

As if, thought Yaz. She wasn't daft. Who knew what might happen? She might find herself catapulted somewhere she wasn't entirely sure about. Or some-when. "I wasn't planning to!"

"If you could mention that to Ryan," the Doctor said. "And to Graham, actually. Honestly, you'd think they were old enough to know better, but some people have sticky fingers. You put a button in front of them, and they have to press it. It's like there are two types of people in the world, those who'll press any passing button, and those who take a moment to think, '*Now, I wonder what might happen if I press this button. . .*' Now, I'm not saying that either one is wrong, I'm just saying that as a general rule, pressing every button that presents itself isn't always the best button-pressing strategy, and that a little common-sense in the face of buttons can go a long way. . ." She stopped, mid-flow. "Buttons? What am I talking about now? How did I get onto buttons? Wasn't I doing something?" She stared at her hands. "Oh yeah, that was it!"

The Doctor's attention went back to the controls. Yaz watched her concentrate: this amazing, exciting, wonderful, marvellous, and – yes, all right – sometimes incomprehensible stranger who had landed in their lives and shaken them up beyond anything Yaz would have imagined possible. She felt a thrill down her spine, and was just about to ask that most magical of questions, *Where now, Doctor?*, when the Doctor pointed to an image that had appeared on the wall.

"Have a look at that."

Yaz looked. It was a rock. Planet-sized, mind you, but definitely a rock. "Um, I see a rock? A big rock?"

"Alien planet, Yaz!" The Doctor laughed. "I've got a feeling about it."

"A feeling?" Yaz's spine tingled again. She peered at the rock. The Doctor adjusted the image. Yaz saw grass, a pebbled beach, the sea gently lapping at the shore… She thought of a bank holiday the family had once had at Scarborough. "Doctor, what do you see? What am I missing?"

"Not sure yet," the Doctor said. "All I know is – we need to look below the surface of things." She grinned. "Shall we go out and have a look?"

"Of course!" Yaz laughed. "What are we waiting for?"

"All right then," said the Doctor. "Let's try parking this thing."

She pulled and twisted at some levers. There was a huge thump, big enough to make Yaz grab for the console and hold on. Another thump. Then a bump. Some more thumping. Then everything went quiet.

"Oops," said the Doctor.

"How many points have you got on your licence?" said Yaz.

"Lost count." The Doctor pushed some buttons. "Now where are those boys? Don't they know there's a whole new great big rock out there?"

Once upon a time there were three friends. They came into the world together, and they grew together, and they knew each other very well. But each one was very different –

hewn from their own stone, as the saying goes. The first was friendly and generous; the second was careful and industrious; and the last of the three was curious about – well, everything really. He liked to explore, and to find out new things, and he liked to look at the world around him and think about what everything meant, and whether he could understand things better.

The world in which these three lived was very beautiful and people were, on the whole, very happy. There weren't all that many of them, and they all knew each other well, and they all looked out for each other. It was a safe and happy world for these three friends to grow up in. The first did very well in life. He made friends easily, and was good company. Best of all, he had a lucky touch. Silver flowed from his hand, as the saying goes, and his expansive nature meant he did not hoard. He discovered that he liked to be generous, and he liked to be able to do favours for people, to be the one they called on when they needed help. He enjoyed life, and he prospered.

The second friend found life harder. She was serious-minded, given to working hard and fretting. When she looked around her, she did not see beauty, but saw tasks to be done, people to be cared for. She saw the world around her and the people around her as charges, as responsibilities, all of which were hers – and that is a big task for anyone. She worried a great deal, and more and more she felt as if the whole world depended on her, and she was not sure that she was enough for the task. And that made her lonely and, sometimes, angry.

As for the third – always looking upwards and outwards – he acquired a reputation as something of an oddity. People put up with him because he was one of their Great Family, and Family is all there is, but the truth was he didn't really fit in. In his youth, he didn't notice much, he was so busy. But as time passed, our friend also became less and less happy. The more he looked at the world around him, the more he understood it, the more he was sure that things weren't right. From watching, and studying, and thinking, he became sure that something was going wrong, badly wrong. So he tried to tell people what he was thinking, and what he was seeing. At first they laughed at him, but, later, they started to become angry with him. Why was he always trying to spoil things? Why was he always talking about how bad things were? Did he want people to be unhappy? He found that even his oldest friends stopped listening. One said that she thought that he should stop, that he was harming the Great Family by insisting on his strange ideas. They quarrelled, and didn't talk to each other again. The other friend offered consolation, and tried to help as much as he could.

But after a while, our friend stopped trying to talk to people, stopped trying to explain. He realised that they didn't want to hear what he had to say. But he didn't give up on his ideas, and he didn't give up believing that someone had to do something. He decided to go travelling, go adventuring, out beyond the beautiful City in which he lived, and up and up, until he found the answers to all his questions. It was a wrench. He was leaving friends and family behind. But he knew he had to go... because somebody had to, before everything was lost... And off he went, very quietly, one day, with a handful of people that he trusted absolutely, and the people he left behind waited and waited, hoping beyond hope that one day he would return safely, and bring answers to all their questions...

The TARDIS doors opened. Yaz held her breath. She loved this moment before a whole new world opened in front of her. She liked the anticipation, the not-knowing, and the endless possibilities. The Doctor went outside, and Yaz followed as quickly as she could. It took a few seconds for her eyes to adjust. At first everything seemed dark, as if she'd walked into a cave, but then Yaz realised that there were lights everywhere, sparkling in the rocks around the group of friends.

Yaz took stock of their surroundings. The TARDIS had come to land in a narrow cleft between two sheer rocky cliffs. There was space in the gap for the TARDIS, and just enough on either side for the friends to get past, one-by-one. The Doctor was already off, and as Yaz made her way round to join the Doctor, she ran her hand along the rock. This close, she could see that it was encrusted with gems and crystals and precious stones, and that these gave off a soft and glimmering light. Yaz looked up again. Far above, the roof of the world was shimmering in the same way, a faint and distant haze.

Behind her, Graham spoke. He sounded very uncertain. "Is it night? Or are we in a cave? I can't tell."

The Doctor led the other three along the cleft and, after a little way, the cliffs parted, allowing them to come out onto a wide flat rocky space. Then they were able to get their first proper look at this new world on which they had landed.

Yaz felt dizzy for a moment, as if everything had tilted slightly. She had to rub her eyes before looking round again. She had a clear view over the rocky plain. Far in the distance, the horizon seemed to curve oddly. Trick of the light? She rubbed her eyes again. She wasn't sure.

"Am I gonna have to get my eyes tested?" Graham said, plaintively.

Yaz nodded her understanding. There was an eerie haze around them, and she couldn't work out where it was coming from. She couldn't see the sun anywhere, or a moon, or anything that might be a source of light.

"Doctor," Ryan called out, from behind. "Are those stars or what?"

He was standing with his hands in pockets, staring upwards at the… sky? Yaz wasn't sure if that was exactly the word. Something didn't seem quite right. She had the oddest feeling that she was looking at a ceiling rather than out into a limitless expanse. But at the same time, there were little glimmers of light speckling overhead. For a moment, Yaz fancied that these were distant lanterns. That couldn't be right. She shook her head and looked again at the lights. Between these the sky seemed to ripple, and here and there she saw longer strands of light, threads linking the points to each other.

"They don't look much like stars," Ryan said.

"What else could they be?" said Graham.

"Let's find out." The Doctor took the sonic out again, and for once didn't wave it around, but stood still, arm outstretched, the sonic pointing upwards. She looked like the conductor of some celestial orchestra, directing the music of the heavens, coaxing sweet music from the ether.

"Huh," she said, at last. "Interesting set of measurements. No, they're not stars. They're lights. Crystalline." She had her thinking face on, eyes screwed up, chewing her bottom lip.

"Doc, when you say lights," said Graham, "what do you mean? Like those precious stones?" He pointed back to the shimmering rock face.

"I don't know," said the Doctor. She grinned and bounced off, calling back over her shoulder, "Shall we put that on our list of things to find out?"

Graham's shoulders slumped. "And we're off."

Ryan patted his arm. "You know you love it really," he said. He nodded ahead, where the Doctor was already striding off, Yaz keeping pace at her side. "Come on, we can't let them get too far ahead. Family honour and all that."

They followed the ridge as it bent round. Yaz couldn't keep her eyes off the shimmering jewels encrusting the rock. They were almost like directions, she thought; signposts, encouraging the friends to follow the path laid out. She thought again about what the Doctor had said, that the stones were partly natural, partly fashioned and shaped in some way. Whose hands had done this, she wondered. What was their purpose?

Suddenly, Ryan stumbled and nearly fell over. Graham was beside him in a shot. "All right, mate?"

"Yeah, I'm fine, no problem." Ryan blinked and shook his head. "Is it just me, or does anyone else feel dizzy? Like everything's bending in the wrong direction?"

"It's not just you," said Yaz. "Ever since I got here, I've felt like things aren't right. My foot goes down and the ground is closer than I expected. It's weird."

"Me too," said Graham, and patted Ryan's arm. "It's not just you. I wonder what it is though. I read about this museum once. They'd built all the walls at a tilt, at weird angles, so that when people came in, they'd get vertigo. Some people would reel about, some people even fall over when they go in."

"Why would anyone do that?" said Ryan.

"I dunno," said Graham. "I think it was to make people think about life in the War. Anyway, this is how it felt, I bet. Like the walls are just at the wrong angle."

Throughout all this, the Doctor had been standing roughly on the same spot, slowly shuffling round, holding the sonic above her head as she went.

"All right, Doctor," said Yaz. "You did your excited-to-be-here face. That turned into your quiet-I'm-using-the-sonic-face. Which turned into the if-this-is-what-I-think-it-is-I'm-even-more-excited face."

The Doctor was now wearing what Yaz thought of as her I'm-not-entirely-sure-I-believe-a-word-you're-saying-to-me face. She said, "Do I really do that many faces?"

"Yes," the others said, in unison.

"What usually happens next," said Ryan, "is that you start bouncing around like Tigger."

"Tigger? Oh well, it could be worse. I could be Piglet. Well, I'm glad someone knows what's going on with this face because I'm nowhere near used to it," the Doctor said. "And, yeah, it *is* exciting, to be honest! We're not *outside* a planet. We're *inside* one."

"How does that work, then?" said Graham.

"Dead easy," said the Doctor. "Your world – most worlds – have a crust and loads of layers around a molten core. Not here. Here there's... a sort of balloon inside, right in the middle. A bubble. An egg shell. Outside, on the planet's crust, it looks like there's nothing. Think what we saw on the surface."

"We didn't see anything on the surface," said Yaz. "Nothing major, anyway."

"That beach looked like it might be nice," said Graham.

"It was nice enough, yeah, but nothing to write home about." The Doctor spread out her hands in delight. "Do you see? *This* is where the world is!"

"So all this – we're *inside* the bubble," said Graham, slowly.

"Keep up, granddad," said Ryan.

"Oi," said Graham, "button it!"

"That's right," said the Doctor. "Inside."

"So that's why everything feels funny," Graham said. "Because it's curving round the wrong way."

"Not *wrong*," said the Doctor. "Just *different*. If someone from here visited your world, they'd not understand why you were all scurrying along on the surface. They'd worry about flying off and they'd want to get inside." She paused, thinking. "I wonder if they even *know* there's a surface..."

"Hold on," said Yaz. "Are we even sure there are people?"

The Doctor looked at her steadily. "Those jewels didn't fashion themselves, Yaz." She pointed ahead. "Come on. Let's look round the other side of the ridge."

They turned the corner—

—And, far in the distance, they saw the City.

"Oh," said Graham, in a very soft voice. "Blimey."

Sheer white towers shot skywards. Anywhere else, Yaz might have thought they were glass skyscrapers, but not here. These were like huge stalagmites, hollowed out, a whole city of crystals. They seemed to shine from within, and here and there white jewels and pale gemstones – sapphire and ruby and topaz and emerald – had been set into the crystal structures to make patterns and decorations, beautiful and intricate mosaics. Light bounced off these from every angle. The whole City shimmered, as if the stone was gently swaying to an alien rhythm. Faintly, distantly, Yaz heard chimes – the music of the City. She breathed out. What they must be like, the people who had created this splendour? How did they see the world? What did they care about, and who were they? Yaz was seized with a great desire to know more about them. *There must be good about them*, she thought, *to make something so beautiful*. She tried to say something, something wise and clever enough to capture how moved she felt at this glorious sight.

"I take back anything bad I might have said about rocks."

The Doctor laughed.

"It's beautiful," said Ryan, gazing at the City with his mouth half-open in delight. "It's really beautiful!"

"Yeah," said Graham, "it really is. Doc, is that city made of diamonds?"

"You know what, Graham, I think it is."

They walked on, steadily. The City beckoned them, but, as they walked, Yaz could not shake a growing sense of unease. The air around them seemed to have become very still.

"Hmm," Yaz said.

She had the Doctor's immediate attention. "What is it?" she said. "What's worrying you?"

"Everything feels weird," Yaz said. "Too still. Stifled. Can you feel it?"

Ryan was nodding. "Yeah, I know what you mean. It feels like there's a storm coming."

"But we're inside," Graham said. "Can there even *be* storms, inside?"

"Who knows what the weather does round here?" the Doctor said. "This place is certainly big enough to have climates."

They walked on further. Yaz found herself thinking, of all things, about a geography lesson at school, about those big waves that could suddenly hit islands, wiping out everything in their path. The first clue people got – and it wasn't much warning – was this strange, breathless calm, before the chaos and destruction… What were they called? Ah, that was it…

"Tsunamis," she said.

"Eh?" said Graham.

"A big wave," said Ryan. He gave Graham a big wave. "Not one of them."

"I know what a tsunami is, Ryan, I just don't know why Yaz is talking about them all of a sudden—"

"The calm before the storm," the Doctor said.

The Doctor stood still. Yaz knew that look – she thought something terrible was about to happen.

"Doctor," said Yaz, urgently, "if something's about to happen, we should get away right now—"

"You're right," the Doctor said. "Come on, back to the TARDIS—"

She swung round, all determination and focus. Yaz, looking ahead, cried out, "Doctor! Don't move!"

The Doctor froze. A few feet in front of her, the ground had started to bubble. It reminded Yaz, weirdly, of the surface of an apple crumble, right out of the oven, the hot thick liquid pushing up and through.

"Move back, all of you," the Doctor said.

Carefully, they inched backwards, away from the rippling ground. As they moved, Yaz saw that there was steam rising from the rocks.

What happened next happened very quickly. One second there was steam, and the next, with a vast roar, white fume shot up in a huge jet. Yaz yelled and jumped backwards.

"Move!" cried the Doctor. "Get back! Get away!"

Yaz sprinted off. Glancing back over her shoulder she saw Ryan stumble. Behind him, the ground was crumbling. Yaz watched in horror to see Graham dash back to get him away from the edge.

"Graham!" she cried. "Be careful!"

Too late. Graham's sudden movement had done exactly what Yaz had feared. Beneath his feet, the ground began to slip away at an alarming rate. With one last shove, Graham sent Ryan flying to safety. But the damage was done. The ground crumbled – and Graham began to slide down, towards the boiling liquid.

Two

Ash had always been something of a loner. Partly that was her nature, which was quiet and inward-looking. Ash liked time alone to think. But a large part of her solitariness was because over the years she got tired of being known first and foremost as her father's daughter. Ash's father had a reputation for saying strange things. People had humoured him to begin with, until they came to realise that he believed in what he was saying. At first they laughed, and then, when he kept insisting that what he said was true, then began to get impatient, and then angry – and then, the worst punishment of all in this small and close-knit world, they gave him the silent treatment.

It had been a hard time. People on the whole were fair, and didn't judge Ash for her father's strange ideas, but she was completely loyal to him. Ash believed in her father – really believed in him. She had watched him work since she was a speck; had sat beside him in his workshop, and seen his ideas emerge and develop and become fully-faceted, like a great and brilliant stone, carefully cut by a master jeweller. Ash knew how sharp her father's mind was. She would never buy friends or a quiet life by laughing at her father behind his back. So on the whole it was much easier to spend time by herself, go out beyond the Diamond City up onto the quiet ridges, and lie on her back looking up at the twinkling lights above, and wonder whether there really was anything more, like her father believed.

Ash's people, as a rule, didn't like being alone. Their world was enclosed, literally, and even in the more distant settlements curving around the great bowl of the world, you weren't out of sight, and you could easily see the bright light of the Diamond City, the heart of the world. The Great Family kept together, and everyone knew who everyone else was, and what their business was, and what their friends and relations' business was, and if it wasn't their business already they made it their business. So this habit of creeping off to be quiet, to be alone, was yet another reason to look at Ash and think that perhaps something wasn't quite right.

And then her father had gone away…

Ash liked it out here. She felt closer to her father. When she was very small, she and her father would come here, and when he had finished collecting samples, and she had helped him organise them and label them, they would walk along the ridge, and sit together and look out at the whole sphere of the world curving around them. The light of the gems around them would gradually fade, as the night cycle began, and her father would point upwards and say, "What can you see, Ash?"

She loved this game, picking out the patterns from the shimmering haze above. One by one she would name the landmarks. First of all, there was the rippling sea that connected the whole of the Great Family to each other. Next she would point out the little rocky islands dotted around that sea, and, as she got bigger, she would tell him their names – Isbiter, with its streams of silver, and Tetziger, the best source of pumice. She would point out the biggest ore-rivers on the islands, and the canals that had been dug, nudging the rivers to make them more useful. She would point out the bigger settlements – the twinkling lanterns of the Topaz encampment, and the three villages around the delta of the Fire River. She would describe to him the great bowl of their world, reaching all around them, and year by year she knew more and more about it, until one day she realised that she knew everything. She knew all the paths and the ways that her people had made and always took. And suddenly she realised just how much of the great sphere of the world was unmapped, was full of places where the Great Family never ventured.

"Dad," she asked "is there anything else?"

"Hmm?" he said. "What do you mean?"

She looked up at the little lights overhead, the signs of her own people on the far side of the sphere of the world. "I mean… is there anywhere else to go?"

He looked at her curiously. "What makes you say that?"

"It's just… sometimes I look up and I think I can see lights, and I can't name them. I don't know which island they're on, and I don't know who's making them. Like there are cracks in the sky—" She saw his expression, and stopped, suddenly. "Dad?"

"So you've noticed that, have you?"

She didn't know what to say. He'd always told her to look carefully, look honestly, not to take things for granted.

"Dad? What is it?"

He didn't answer at first. He went quiet, and seemed to forget that she was there. But she trusted him. He always tried to find a way to answer her questions.

"The thing is, Ash," he said, and a curious glimmer had come into his eyes, like a smouldering fire, "this can't be all there is. There must be something more. Something *beyond*... Something lights the rocks around us. Something causes the night cycle, the day cycle. Something must be happening to make those cracks appear, and behind them there must be some source of light…"

She had shivered to hear this. What else was there but the world? Could there really be something beyond this small, safe, well-known sphere of theirs? She pressed him again and again over the years, but what that something was, exactly, her father would never quite say. Protecting her, she guessed. Not until she was older, and read his essays and notes, did she realise the full extent of her father's beliefs. That there were holes in the roof of the world through which light came through, and that beyond the roof was the surface of the world, and beyond that was...

Infinity.

Did she believe this too? Did she believe him? Ash had tried to imagine infinity, many times, and she couldn't. But she was wise enough to know that this didn't mean her father must be wrong. Whatever the limitations of her own mind and her own immediate experience, Ash saw no reason to believe that those were the boundaries of reality. This world, her own world, was very beautiful, and contained wonders. Why could there not be even more?

Ash sighed. She wished those days could come back, of coming here with her father, and watching the world as it always had been and always would. But things had been changing for a long time, all around her, however much everyone wanted them to stay the same. It was what had finally made him leave. His careful observations, gathered over the years, his notes and records, dating back well before the start of Ash's life. They all pointed him to a clear conclusion: that the sphere of the world was changing. He had tried to tell this to people, but they were scared of what it might mean, and didn't know what to do. They pretended it wasn't happening, and when he insisted, they got angry and told him to be quiet. There was talk of banishment, the worst punishment that could be handed out, to send someone away from the Great Family. In the end, her father had taken matters into his own hands.

"They won't believe me when I tell them what's happening, Ash," he had said. "But it is happening. The steaming pools, the hot jets, the ground crumbling beneath us—"

"The cracks in the sphere," she said.

"Those most of all," he said. "Someone has to find out what's happening."

And so he had gone – he and a few friends – and a hundred, two hundred nights and days had past, and Ash had heard nothing...

The lights of the gems were darkening steadily, signifying that the night cycle was coming. It was time to return to the City. Ash knew that people were keeping an eye on her – for her own good, of course – and she didn't want questions or trouble. She jumped lightly to her feet. She had two ways to go home: the high way, along the ridge and down the Stairs, or else she could climb down now into the Narrow Cleft, and walk home along the plain. She was looking over the edge of the ridge, considering the climb, when she saw something she had never seen before.

First there was the colour – blue, blue as any lapis lazuli – and then there was the shape. Big. Solid, like a box. And then came the *sound*...

Ash gasped. A big blue box had appeared from *nowhere*...

The box opened, and creatures came out. Strange creatures.

At first, Ash did not know what to think. Then her heart leapt for joy.

"People," she whispered. "They're *people*!"

Her next thought was how strange they looked. Were they wearing costumes? Were they wearing armour? She could see nothing remotely usual about them, could not guess the stone or ore from which they had been hewn.

They walked along the Narrow Cleft, talking to each other. Ash could not quite hear what they were saying, but something about them made her heart open to them. They were curious, stopping to touch the rocks as they passed, and when she caught a glimpse of their strange, mobile faces, they seemed to be enchanted by everything they saw. She scrambled along the ridge, tracking them, hoping they would take the path that would give them view of the City. She wanted to see what they would think of that!

When they got there, Ash's heart filled with pride to see their looks of delight and amazement at her beautiful home. She followed them as they walked on, looking round, taking stock of her world, and she began to form the words that she would say to welcome them. And most of all, she wished her father had been there, sitting with her as he had done so many times, for so many years, before suspicion and mistrust had made him leave. She wanted to cry out to him: *It's true! It's all true! Everything you ever told me was true!*

These new and precious strangers – all the proof he had ever needed.

Then she saw a glint of emerald in the distance. She opened her mouth to cry out to the strangers to warn them—

And then the ground crumbled beneath their feet.

Graham was scrabbling at the ground, trying to get some sort of hold. Ryan and Yaz, dashing forwards, each took one of his arms, pulling him as hard as they could. Yaz felt the stones crumbling beneath her too.

"Come on..." she hissed to herself. "Come *on!*"

With one last, almighty heave, they pulled Graham onto safe ground. He jumped to his feet, and the four friends dashed away from the seething pool of hot liquid, to safety. Graham fell on the ground, wheezing. He gasped out, "Shoe!"

"You're welcome," said Ryan.

"Not bless you! Shoe!" Graham pointed at his sock. "I've lost my shoe!"

"Here you are," said Yaz, handing him his shoe.

"Thanks, Yaz love." Graham slipped the shoe on, and stood up. Carefully, he peered back towards the new river that had opened up.

"Don't worry," said Ryan. "You're not cooked yet."

Graham turned to the Doctor. "Are we staying here long? I don't fancy becoming roast dinner."

The Doctor sighed. "Well, the TARDIS is on the other side of *that...*" She pointed at the steaming river that lay in front of him.

"Oh," said Graham. "That's a problem, isn't it?"

"If we want to leave here at some point, yes, yes it is," the Doctor confirmed. She looked at her companions in turn. "Who packed the rope?"

They looked back at her.

"Ryan? Rope?"

"Rope?" Ryan said. "Nope."

"Ah. Well. Perhaps we can find one. Or *make* one..." The Doctor looked around, thoughtfully, as if considering what rocks she might use to fashion into a rope, and how this might in fact be done. "Hmm," she said, then, brightly: "Oh! Better idea!"

"Go on," said Ryan.

The Doctor pointed into the distance. "We'll ask them to lend us one."

They all looked over to where she was pointing. Yaz had to squint, but – yes, they were definitely there, two figures running towards them, along the rocks.

"Doctor," she said, "are you *sure* about these two?"

"Am I sure they're friendly? Of course I'm sure! Everyone needs rope. If there's hills and holes and people, and those people have arms, and sometimes even when they don't, then there's rope. And then there's the people made of rope, and the ones made of yarn, or string... There was that macramé world I went to once, or was that a dream...? Macramé World doesn't sound very likely when you say it out loud, does it? I'm *sure* I did, though... Anyway, there's always *rope*! It's practically a universal law. In fact, there's so much rope out there," the Doctor was in full flight now, "that there should be a name for it. How about Rope's Law...? No! I know!" She clicked her fingers. "The Doctor's Law. Yeah, I like that, that's good, I won't forget that—"

"Doctor," said Yaz, patiently, "I wasn't talking about the rope. I was worrying about whether these people running towards us mean us well."

"Might just be me," said Ryan, "but I think it's something to do with the way they're shouting at us and waving those big sticks above their heads."

"Can't be sticks, Ryan, there are no trees."

"Rods, then," said Ryan.

"Truncheons," said Yaz.

"Things they're gonna whack us with," said Graham, "for which we do not yet have a name."

"Yeah, those are better," said the Doctor.

The two figures were close now. As they approached the friends, they slowed to a walk, coming to a halt five or six feet away. Yaz could see them properly, and it almost took her breath away. They were rock, or so it seemed; made from rock, but supple – moving, breathing, *living*… Their flesh – no, that wasn't right, thought Yaz – their shells or carapaces were encrusted with bright stones and gems, not as decoration, but as part of what they were. The light refracted off them as they moved. One shimmered with pinks and reds, like rubies; the other was shades of blue, like sapphires. They had one thing in common: both of them, on their chests, had a single stone as an ornament – a green emerald.

They looked at the friends; the friends looked back.

"What on earth *are* they?" Graham whispered.

"We're not *on* Earth," said the Doctor, with a sigh.

"Oh my days," said Ryan, with a nervous laugh. "They look like… rock goblins!"

"They're beautiful," said Yasmin, softly.

"They're *people*," said the Doctor. "And we can talk to people. Get to know them. Find out what makes them tick." She clapped her hands together. "Right. Let me handle this. I'm great with aliens. Look how well I get on with you lot." She waved over at them. "Hello! How are you? Have either of you by any chance got a rope?"

One of them – the sapphire one – moved forwards. She – or he, or it, Yaz couldn't say for sure and wouldn't like to guess – lifted up the rod it was carrying. Close up, it looked like a long crystal wand. Yaz wondered if it fired anything; jewel-bullets or quartz-rays. She wasn't keen on finding out.

"Who are you?" said the sapphire-person.

The Doctor waved. "Hello! I'm the Doctor. These are my mates. Friends. Fam."

The sapphire one pointed the wand at the steaming river. "Why did you create these?"

"What?" said Ryan. "You think we smashed the ground open on purpose?"

"We wouldn't do that," said Yaz. "We were nearly caught in it!"

"I almost got boiled!" said Graham. "Steamed! Cooked! Alive! Me!"

Sapphire looked at him coolly, then turned to talk to the ruby creature. They spoke softly, but with great urgency. The Doctor watched them carefully. "This is a disappointing start." She turned to the others and gave them an embarrassed smile. "I hate saying this," she said. "Such a cliché. Ashamed of myself, really. But you get a hunch about this kind of thing and so I think we should—"

The walking rocks stopped talking and began to move closer, lifting up their sticks. Rods. Truncheons. Things they were going to whack with.

"*Run!*"

The friends started to run.

Ash had known from the moment she saw the green stones glinting in the distance that trouble was on the way. The new arrivals were the Greenwatch, tasked to observe other members of the Great Family and report back to their leader, Emerald, of any unusual behaviour. Ash's father had been plagued by them in the days leading up to his disappearance: it had seemed to Ash at one point that she couldn't turn around without seeing an emerald nearby. And now she was caught in a dilemma: if she warned the strangers, it would bring attention to her presence here, up on the ridge, and then there would be questions about why she was there, what had brought her all this way from the City...

Ash chose caution. She lay flat on the ground, watching anxiously as these strange new people pulled themselves away from the seething pool, and then in alarm as the Greenwatch approached them. She watched the foursome run, but they were on unfamiliar terrain, and it wasn't long before the Greenwatch caught up with them. Soon enough they were being marched off across the rocky plain.

Ash stood up. The night cycle was well underway; the only light came from the gently glowing stones in the rocks, and from the distant haze on the other side of the sphere of the world, far away and up above. She heard the soft chirrup of jet-flies, whispering to welcome the night and send bright dreams. The Greenwatch and their prisoners became greying figures in the distance, and soon could not be distinguished in the gloom. Ash did not worry. She was fairly certain she knew where they were heading, and that she could find her way there. What she had to do in the meantime was make sure that she was not seen.

She walked slowly round the ridge, and came to the Small Steps. She slipped down these to come down onto the plain. This news, the news of these arrivals – this was significant. This was important. The Greenwatch would have instructions, and chief amongst these would be not to let this news out. They would certainly not want to risk taking the strangers through the walkways of the

Diamond City. They would hold them somewhere, and go to get help and instructions.

Ash sat down, her back against the sheer face of the rock. The night wore on. Soon she was invisible in the darkness. In the distance, the city-chimes rang, and then, later, rang again. Ash sat, and listened, and watched. At last, her patience was rewarded, and she saw a glint of green coming back through the darkness. She pressed back against the rock and did not move. The Greenwatch passed by with no idea that she was there. She waited until the chimes sounded the second portion. And then quietly, ever so quietly, she slipped off into the night.

Yaz sighed and thumped the flat of her hand against the rock. Sapphire and Ruby, as the friends had decided to call them, had proven themselves able to move very quickly over the rock. They'd lifted up their wands and threatened to use them. The Doctor, deciding she didn't want to find out what the creatures might do, had stopped them all from running on any further. After that they'd been marched a little way, out across a limestone plain. Everything was getting darker, and Yaz had started to worry, when suddenly they'd stopped, in the middle of nowhere.

There'd been a hole in the ground, and their captors had made them jump down into it. Then Yaz watched in horror as they lifted a large flat stone over the top of the hole. It fell into place with a *thud*. There was a small hole in it, through which they could look out and watch the light fade.

"Rope," muttered the Doctor darkly, looking up at the hole. "I'm just saying. I'm going to have to make one of you rope monitor. I can't think of everything…"

Yaz sighed and looked round. There was room enough for the four of them, barely, and she was willing to bet a small fortune that Graham snored. Actually, she was willing to put money on all three of the others snoring. Yaz didn't snore, no matter what her sister said.

The Doctor was now making herself comfortable. She sat down and rested her back against the wall. She flicked out her sonic, and took a reading. "From arrival to dungeon in…" She counted under her breath. "Just under an hour. Oh, that's *rubbish*," she said. "That's miles off my personal best."

Ryan, pacing the tiny space, came to a halt by her. "You're not very worried."

"Why worry?" said the Doctor. "Seen one dungeon, seen them all."

"Why worry?!" said Ryan. "We've been captured by walking talking rocks!"

"I thought they looked more like jewels," said Yaz softly. "They're like nothing I've ever seen before…"

"They've stuck us in here!" said Ryan. "Anyway, rocks, people – what difference does it make?"

"It makes a lot of difference." The Doctor was very serious now. "For one thing, we can talk to people – whatever they're made of. Flesh, rock, or lace."

"Lace?" Graham laughed. "Really?"

"Yeah, really!" The Doctor beamed. "Fourth moon of Galatiasaritius Minor. Maybe we'll go there next. Just don't ask for antimacassars. And, for another thing," the Doctor turned back to Ryan, "these creatures probably have a good reason for being afraid of us. Because that's all they are – afraid of us." She smiled. "I know, I know, we're *gorgeous*. But to them – well, who knows what kind of nightmare we are? I mean, we're made of *meat*. Have you ever stopped to think about that?" She stopped, and thought, and shuddered. "*Meat*."

"All right," said Ryan, with only the tiniest touch of the sulks. "I get the point."

"To be fair to you, though," said the Doctor, patting his arm, "we haven't tried to lock them up – and nor would we. Would we?"

"No," said Graham. "'Course not!"

"Thank you," said Ryan, with dignity. "That was my *point*."

"All right, gang," said Yaz. "Can we get down to business? Cave. Stone. How do we get past that and up and out? What about your sonic screwdriver, Doctor?"

"It's not great on rocks," the Doctor admitted. "Let me have a think."

They waited. Time passed. After a little while, they realised the Doctor had nodded off. "Oi," said Ryan, tapping the Doctor's leg with his toe, "we're still locked in a dungeon."

"Hmm? Oh yeah. Sorry. It's dark, though, isn't it?"

"It *is* dark," said Ryan, patiently.

"You get to my age, you don't pass up the chance for a nap. That," said the Doctor, "is the sum total of my wisdom."

"I can second that," said Graham, with feeling.

"Honestly, you two," said Yaz. "Focus. Stay awake. Dungeon. Escape from. Thoughts. Ideas. Plans."

"We could dig our way out," said Graham. "Like in that film... What was it? Your nan loved it, Ryan."

The Shawshank Redemption," said Ryan. "And it took him over twenty years."

"Ah," said Graham. "Climb?"

"I may have mentioned this already," said the Doctor, "but none of you thought to bring any rope."

"There is that," said Graham, peaceably. He looked like he was settling down for the night too.

"No digging, no climbing, no sonicking – what *are* we going to do?" said Yaz.

"Oh, don't worry," said the Doctor, cheerfully. "Something always comes up." She looked up at the stone overhead and waved. "Hello! Who are you?"

Yaz looked up too. A face was peering through the hole in the rock: a jet-black face with silvery flecks like mica. Yaz wondered again what the right word was for the skin of a living rock – crust, maybe? Travelling with the Doctor made you rethink everything, she thought, right down to the right words to use.

"It's OK," the Doctor said. "We're nice. Friendly. I'm the Doctor, by the way. What's your name?"

"I'm Ash," said the alien. "Are you aliens?"

A smile spread across the Doctor's face. In the dark she shone, like diamonds. "They are," she said. "I'm not. Do you have any rope?"

"Of course," said Ash. "Who goes out without rope?"

"Oh, blimey," said Graham. "We'll never hear the last of that."

Three

Three

Once Ash had pulled the stone cover away from the hole, the rope did indeed come in handy. They came out one-by-one, lightest first, so that there were more of them to help pull out Graham and then Ryan at the end. Yaz rolled the rope up again, taking the chance to examine it as it ran through her hands. It was thinner than she expected, so thin that she might not have been happy to be pulled up on it had she been aware, but it was strong, very strong, and felt slightly sticky to touch. She wondered what it was made of. She hadn't, as yet, seen any sort of plants or shrubs to use to make fibres. And now that she thought about it – what kind of *wildlife* was there here? With rocks for people, what could the *animals* be like? Rocks, but with teeth? She shuddered and decided not to mention this.

The friends shook themselves off, checked for scrapes and bruises, and then turned to thank their saviour. She was slighter in build than the others they had already met, but still manifestly the same species. She gleamed jet black in the half-light, and when she moved, flecks of mica shimmered all over her body.

"Hey," said the Doctor, "thanks!"

"You're very welcome," said Ash. She studied each of them one by one, with strange unblinking eyes, and then she shook her head. "I have so many questions—"

"Me too," said the Doctor. "Those pools that appear suddenly. They're getting to be a problem, aren't they?"

"—but first," said Ash, calmly, "I think we should get away from here. The Greenwatch will certainly be coming back, and they may well bring others."

"Oh yeah," said the Doctor. "Probably wise. Greenwatch?"

"The Eyes of Emerald," Ash said.

"Right," said the Doctor.

"Sounds a bit secret policey to me," said Graham.

"Yeah," said the Doctor. "Ash – where should we go?"

"I know a place," Ash said. "Somewhere safe."

The friends conferred briefly. "Doc," said Graham, "what about the TARDIS? Shouldn't we check it's all right?"

"You're keen to leave, aren't you?" said Ryan.

"In my defence, that liquid was *very* hot," said Graham.

"I think we should go with Ash," said Yaz. "Something is happening, isn't it, Doctor?"

The Doctor nodded. "I'd like to find out more."

Ryan was up for it; Graham, with a sigh, fell in with the general plan. Ash, politely, said, "We should go now. They'll be coming back as soon as they can."

"Lead on," said the Doctor.

Ash turned to go, and the friends followed. At first, she led them back the way they had been brought by the

Greenwatch. As they walked, Yaz realised that the darkness was beginning to lift. Faint light was filtering through the rocks all round them.

The Doctor quizzed Ash. "So these eruptions," she said. "They've been happening a lot, haven't they?"

"They have," said Ash. "They started years ago – very rare, at first, but they've become more and more frequent. The liquid – it's horrible!" She shuddered. "It froths and boils, and it kills on touch! When it touches someone – it's awful!"

"I see," said the Doctor. "Anything else?"

"What do you mean?" said Ash.

"There've been other changes too, haven't there?" said the Doctor.

Ash stared at her, dumbfounded. "How do you *know* that?" she asked. "It took my father *years...*"

"Oh, I'm a good guesser," said the Doctor. "No, that's not right. I take care to look around, and then I try to work out what it might all mean. So – go on. Tell me what your father found out."

Ash hesitated. Yaz got the impression that she didn't talk about all this very often.

"What I'm about to say," said Ash, "can get me in a lot of trouble."

"Trouble? From saying things?" The Doctor frowned. "Not sure I like the sound of that. Don't worry, Ash – all I want is to understand what's happening."

Yaz watched a struggle pass over Ash's features. "You can trust us," she said. "And the Doctor might be able to help."

Slowly, Ash nodded. "All right, but please, we must be careful. Things are getting cooler – I'll show you when we get to where we're going. And that means that the seas are shrinking." Ash held out her hands in despair. "It's been going on for years now, and we don't know why. We all know it's happening – even Emerald, however much she denies it. We just don't understand *why*!"

Ash sounded so frightened that Yaz's heart went out to her. How scary this must be. Everything changing, and nobody knowing the cause.

"Hang on," said Ryan, "if all this has been going on ages, then those big rock-guys know it can't be us who caused that pool."

"I don't think they cared either way," said Graham. "They're afraid, and they want someone to blame. We're different. We'll do."

"There's that," said Ash, "and there are some other reasons too."

"Doctor," said Yaz, slipping up alongside her, and keeping her voice very quiet, "you know what the liquid is, don't you?"

"Yes," said the Doctor, softly. "I think so."

"So?"

"Have a guess, Yaz," said the Doctor.

"Is this a good time for guessing games?"

"It's always a good time to come up with an idea and test it. Go on, Yaz. Tell me what you think."

Yaz thought. They were inside this world, however strange that might seem, but she knew what the surface was like. She'd seen it on the TARDIS scanners. There'd been pebbled beaches. Pebbled beaches, along shores. "It's sea water, isn't it?"

The Doctor smiled at her, with pride. "I knew you'd work it out. Yes, sea water. Somehow it's getting through, getting through the shell or the skin of the bubble these people live in. And it's happening more often... Imagine if something cracked the shell beyond repair. This place would flood – fill with water..."

Yaz shuddered. It didn't bear thinking about. "So what's causing it?"

"Not sure yet," the Doctor said. "Lots more questions yet. Ash," she said, more loudly, "your dad sounds like he has his head screwed on the right way. Can we meet him?"

The light in Ash's eyes dimmed. "He's gone," she said, sadly.

"Oh, Ash, I'm sorry," said the Doctor.

"What happened to him?" said Yaz.

"Nothing happened," said Ash. "He... he went away."

"Where to?" Yaz said.

"I don't know," Ash said, sadly. "He'd given up trying to make people listen to him. He said he had to go and find proof of what was happening – something that would make people sit up and listen. He and some friends left – nearly two hundred days ago. He could be anywhere. Lost on the White Way, for all I know. I haven't heard anything since the day he left."

Again, Yaz felt a rush of sympathy. Sometimes her family was so in-your-face that she wished they'd all go away and leave her alone – but she knew she'd be devastated if that happened for real. Like the world had broken apart.

"He'll come back, I know he will," Ash said, bravely. "He has to. He's the only one who can help us."

Yaz glanced over at the Doctor. "Not any more."

They walked on for a long time. The world around them became lighter, although, of course, Yaz couldn't see any sun. Most of the light came from the rocks, from the gems and crystals encrusting them. "Feels like daytime," she said, "but how?"

"I think some light from the surface must get through," the Doctor. "This planet is still spinning, turning one face to its sun and then another. Some of that filters through – and that's what makes the gems light up. Look up now."

The friends stopped to look up at the far side of the sphere. It was darker there now, just a few pinpricks of light here and there. "What are those?" said Ryan.

"Our furthest settlements," Ash said. "Lanterns from our people on the far side of the sphere. It's a long way for them to be – the furthest any of us have ever gone. We like to stay close to each other." She smiled at the Doctor. "Yes, there's natural light here from the rocks, but that's not all. We can fashion gems and other stones to give out light and warmth." Her voice went proud. "My father did that."

Graham was still looking up. "What are those thin threads?" he said. "I'd say they were shooting stars, if I didn't know better."

Ash sighed. "We don't know. They weren't there a few thousand days ago. There seem to be more and more of them as the days go past."

42

Yaz glanced at the Doctor. She was holding the sonic screwdriver up and frowning. Then she shook her head, and walked on.

As the day got brighter, they came to the edge of the ridge along which they had been walking, and looked out over a bleak landscape.

"Blimey," said Graham. "This is worse than Yorkshire."

"Eh," said Yaz. "Less of that."

"What is this place, Ash?" said the Doctor.

"All this used to be sea," said Ash, sadly.

"Sea?" said Ryan. "You mean water?"

"Not water," said the Doctor. "My guess would be lava. A lava sea! It must have been beautiful," the Doctor said, and then gave a wry smile. "If ever-so-slightly hostile to our kind of life."

"You bet! I saw that Mary Beard thing on the telly. Pompeii, you know? It was horrible!" Graham stared out at the lost sea. "Lava, eh? I wouldn't fancy paddling in that."

"No," said the Doctor. "Not much fun – unless you're a rock person. Ash, what was it like here, before this happened?"

"It *was* beautiful," said Ash. Her eyes shone with the memory. "The rocks were so supple, so fluid... The colours melted from white hot to crimson and all the way back again. And the creatures! Hosts and hosts of ember-flies, skating close to the rocks, and then the sea would shift and they would fly upwards in huge waves ..."

"Like a flock of starlings," murmured Yaz.

"You could dig into the lava and pull out fresh gems, still hot in the hand, and you could squeeze them into shape, turn them into dolls or playthings or ornaments, and then leave them to one side to cool while you hunted for more... Or you could take the stone boats out and lie back in them and bask in the heat rising from the lava..." Her face went said. "And now all that's left is this."

They stood and looked across the empty land, the rock bare and cracking.

"A desert," said Graham. "It's not right, is it? Why can't people take care of things, eh?"

"I'm not sure this is entirely the fault of the people here," said the Doctor.

"No," said Ash, "but I think we could do a better job of understanding what's happening."

"There seems to be a lot of denial going on," said Ryan.

"Worse than that," said Ash. "You get into trouble for trying to say what we can all see. My father was mocked for years, and that was bad enough, but I don't think Emerald would let him get away with even saying those things these days."

Yaz glanced at the Doctor. She didn't look happy.

"No," murmured the Doctor. "No, that's not right at all. Emerald, eh? There's always *someone* trying to stop people doing the right thing..."

"Something has to change," said Ash. "Otherwise – I don't think we'll survive this."

The Doctor smiled at her. "Change," she said, "is what I'm all about. Come on – we still have a way to walk, don't we?"

Ash nodded. "A little way."

She led them down the ridge onto what had once been the seashore. They skirted along the edge of the old coast and then back inland. After a while, sheer black cliffs began to rise on either side, until they were walking through a narrow cleft in the rock. Yaz ran her fingertips along the black stone, and soft shards of silver came away. This place seemed so hard, so barren, she thought; but at closer glance everything was delicate and finely wrought. The Doctor was right: look beneath the surface and you so often found wonders.

Ryan sighed. "I don't want to be the one to ask this, but are we nearly there yet?"

"Nearly," said Ash.

"Hang on in there, soldier," said Graham, patting Ryan on the back.

Ash was as good as her word. Overhead, the cliffs met, forming an arch over the narrow tunnel that led them downwards for a while. And then, suddenly, the space ahead of them opened out, and they stepped inside a vast and glittering cave.

"Wow," said Ryan. "OK. Right. Yeah, the walk was worth it."

The cavern they had entered was filled with treasures. A long stone table ran the length of the room, and it seemed to Yaz that every inch of its surface was covered; there were gemstones, and huge rocks, and glass domes with strange specimens inside. The walls were covered with glowing crystals whose colours gently shifted up and down the spectrum. At the far end of the room, there was an alcove in which long thin white crystals hung from the rocky roof. And the whole room seemed to hum, ever so gently, and sweetly.

"Wow," said Ryan. "This is what a wizard's study would look like. *Gandalf's* study."

"You and your daft films," said Yaz, although she knew exactly what he meant.

"Yaz," Ryan said, "we're inside a planet with a bunch of rock people. Those 'daft films'," he did the scare quotes, "are better than TripAdvisor."

"What is this place, Ash?" said the Doctor.

"This is – or was – my father's laboratory. Where he did his studies."

"Scientist, huh?" said Ryan.

"I don't know what that means," said Ash.

"Curious," said Graham. "Liked to ask questions. Liked to find out answers."

"Oh!" said Ash. "Yes! That's him exactly."

"Scientist," said the Doctor, with a nod of her head. "Good, good…"

Graham was peering at something on a table. "Er, what's this?"

The friends gathered round. "Wow." The Doctor was entranced.

On the table, there was a dome of transparent crystal, filled with heaps of rocks and tiny gems. Skittering around these was a small creature, about six inches long, with a brownish hide encrusted with red gems, and the most incredible…

"Teeth," said Ryan. "It has teeth."

"When they were handing out teeth," said Yaz, "they did a good job with this little guy."

"You could do someone a mischief with teeth like that," said Graham.

The creature's beady eyes flashed a malevolent red glare up at them.

"What *is* this thing, Ash?" said Graham.

"That's a ruby rat," said Ash.

"It's beautiful!" said the Doctor.

Ash was laughing. "You sound like my father! Most people call them vermin!"

"That's not nice," said the Doctor. "What have ruby rats ever done to them?"

"Do you want a list?" said Ash, with a smile.

"Poor thing," said the Doctor. She reached forwards and lifted up the dome. The rat didn't waste any time, scampering for freedom and diving for cover behind what looked to be a huge heap of diamonds. Ryan shouted out, Graham yelped, and Yaz grabbed his arm.

The Doctor burst out laughing. "Go on, little guy, run for the hills!"

Ash was unperturbed. She picked up a handful of tiny crystals, coaxed the creature out from its lair, grabbed it by the scruff of its neck, and trapped it back beneath the dome. "I'd be grateful if we kept it in here," she said. "They really can do a lot of damage and, besides, my father's very fond of it and would be sad if it escaped."

The friends peered in again, watching the beast crunch away at the crystals. "Wow, though!" said the Doctor. "Look at those *teeth*!"

"I said, didn't I?" said Ryan. "I said you should look at the teeth."

"You know," said Ash, politely, "I do have a few questions."

"Me too," said the Doctor. "Tell you what – you go first, then I'll have a turn."

"All right." Ash took a deep breath. "You're not from this planet, are you?"

"That's right," said the Doctor. "We're not from this planet. We're not even from the same planet as each other." She glanced at her friends. "Well, they are. I'm from somewhere else again." She studied Ash carefully. "Is that OK?"

"Is it OK?" Ash burst out laughing. "It's wonderful! It's *amazing*!"

The Doctor grinned at her. "I knew I was going to like you!"

"Oh, it's everything my father always dreamed of!" said Ash, clapping her hands together. "All coming true! He thought – he said there were holes in the roof of the world, and that he'd seen bright lights coming through, and that meant that this world wasn't all there was, but that if you dug through the stone far enough you'd find there was another surface up there, high, high above… But everyone just *laughed*…" Ash's face went sad. "He was right, though, wasn't he? There *is* more up there."

"Ash," said Graham, "you've not even seen the half of it."

"It's pretty cool," agreed Ryan.

"It's amazing," said Yaz. "Travelling with the Doctor is… amazing."

The Doctor crinkled up her nose. "Aw, thanks guys! That's one of the nicest things anyone's ever said to me."

She put her hand on Ash's arm. "So your old dad taught you to look up and imagine what might be up there? I'm sure I'd like your father, Ash. I hope I get to talk to him. Did he leave you any messages, any clues?"

"There are his notes..." Ash said, doubtfully. "But he always wrote in code..." She was about to say more, when they heard a chiming sound. They all stopped dead.

"What's that?" said Ryan.

"It's an alarm system that my father set up," Ash said. "To let him know if anyone was approaching."

"Could the Greenwatch have found us?" the Doctor said. "Do they know about this place?"

Ash looked scared. "My father kept it very secret... I suppose it's possible someone followed us?" She glanced round the group of friends. "Keep quiet. I'll go and see."

She left the room. After a minute or two, they head muffled voices.

"Doc," whispered Graham, glancing worriedly at Ryan. "Should we be going?"

"Not yet," the Doctor said.

"These people need our help," Yaz said.

"I don't think we can hold back climate change, Yaz love," Graham said, doubtfully.

"Somebody has to!" said Yaz.

"Ash is taking her time," said Ryan. "Do you think she needs some help?"

He had barely finished speaking when a figure crashed into the room. A giant, Yaz thought at first; a huge, purplish creature with a jagged row of crystals standing up from its brow.

"*Great* crest!" said the Doctor. "Love it! Look at that! That's punchy. Let me guess – quartz?"

The giant stood stock still and blinked at her. "What? How did you know my name?"

"I like rocks," said the Doctor, simply. "And I like to know the names of things."

"She's sort of Gandalfy," said Ryan, helpfully, then his face fell. "Oh, I don't suppose you've seen those films."

"Films," said Quartz, rolling the word round in his mouth like a pebble. "Films."

"Pictures. Movies. Flicks." Ryan shook his head. "You know what? Don't worry about it."

"So, Quartz," the Doctor said. "Are you friend or foe?"

His eyes gleamed at her. "That depends."

"Depends on what?" said Graham.

"On you," said Quartz.

"Oh," said Graham. "Fair enough."

"He's a friend," Ash said, firmly. "Quartz, why are you here?"

"I heard a rumour," Quartz said. "Back in the City… Strangers, seen out on the Plain. Strange creatures, like walking mushrooms."

"*Mushrooms*?" said Graham.

The Doctor's eyes danced. "I suppose we do look a bit, well, *mushroomy*. To the uninitiated."

"So you're not mushrooms?" said Quartz.

"I am most certainly not!" said Graham. "Can't speak for the others, mind you—"

"So you heard a rumour, Quartz," said the Doctor. "And you came… here? Lucky guess, eh?"

"Anything out of the ordinary usually leads back to Ash and her father. And here you are." Quartz studied each of the friends carefully, in turn. "Funny looking bunch, aren't you?"

They settled into the low chairs around the room. Quartz couldn't keep his eyes off them. Fair enough, thought Yaz; she could hardly keep her eyes off him.

"So Basalt was right after all," Quartz said, and began to laugh.

"Basalt?" asked Graham.

"My father," said Ash. "Quartz is one of his oldest friends, and he's been a great help to us over the years. Helped my father get resources so he could carry out his studies."

"His patron, eh?" said the Doctor. "Very generous."

Quartz smiled. "I've tried."

"He's very well connected," said Ash.

"Hmm," said the Doctor. "Yeah."

Yaz, watching the Doctor carefully, thought, *I wonder why she doesn't like him.*

"What shall we do, Quartz?" said Ash.

"We can't take them to the city. The mood there is..." Quartz shook his head.

"What's happened?" Ash said quietly.

Quartz looked very bleak. "Another pool. In the Great Curve, this time."

"Oh no," whispered Ash.

"It was horrific," Quartz said, his voice clipped.

"What does that mean?" said Graham, uncertainly.

"The Great Curve is the area around the Diamond City," Ash explained. "It's where most of our people live."

"And one of those big pools opened up there?" Ryan shuddered. "Horrible."

"People don't survive if the liquid touches them," said Quartz. "It's dreadful to see."

"Wait a moment," said Ash. "I'll show you."

She went over the room and came back holding a pale blue stone, about the size of a grapefruit. Gently she warmed it between her cupped hands, and the friends watched in amazement as images began to appear within.

"Oh, that's clever," said the Doctor. "Some sort of holocrystal... Very nice, Ash. Your dad has done some brilliant work."

"Doctor," said Yaz, bleakly. "Look."

They watched as the scene unfolded. A small group of rock people, walking along together, were suddenly stopped short as a jet of water shot up in front of them, catching two of them full in its spray. Yaz watched in horror as they dashed away from the steam, their hard shells blistering and cracking. "No," she cried. "That's terrible!"

"It scars us and melts us," said Ash, unhappily. "Doctor, you know what this liquid is, don't you?"

"Yes," the Doctor said. "It's seawater."

Ash shook her head. "I don't know what that means."

"Let me explain," said the Doctor. "So – assume everything your father told you was right. Where you live – your world – it's a huge hollow sphere, right in the middle of a much bigger sphere. When you push through the rocks of that sphere, when you dig as you would say, you really do come out on the surface of the outside sphere."

As the Doctor spoke, Ash's smile grew bigger and bigger. Quartz, Yaz noticed, was giving nothing away.

"It's amazing, isn't it?" the Doctor said. "When you get to the very top, to the surface – well, there's a lot going on there, even on a nice quiet polite little planet like yours. There's land-masses – the tops of the rocks, basically – and between them are the seas. Like your lava seas, but filled with a different kind of liquid – water. That liquid, that water, is leaking through down here somehow." She frowned. "I'm not quite sure why yet. Anyway, when it does, it gets super-heated, and it bursts through the shell of your sphere, and out into your world. We need to stop that from happening."

"And the rest?" said Ash. "The shrinking seas? The cooling down?"

"All connected somehow," said the Doctor. "We need to take a closer look."

"All this time," Quartz said softly. "I thought some of what Basalt was saying might be true, but…" He laughed. "Well, look at you all! You're so…"

"Alien?" suggested Ryan.

"So what do you think we should do, Quartz?" Ash said.

"I don't know." He looked worriedly at the Doctor and her friends. "We can't hide them here forever—"

"Yeah, well, I don't plan on hiding here at all," said the Doctor.

"It's not as simple as that," said Quartz.

"People say that to me all the time," said the Doctor. "And you know what? It usually is pretty simple." She turned to Ash. "I want to speak to your father. Find out what he's learned."

"That isn't possible," said Quartz. "He left ages ago."

"We can follow him," the Doctor said.

Quartz shook his head. "That isn't—"

"Possible," said the Doctor. "Yeah, I know. But I think we should try. Ash, did your father leave a map? Details of what route he was planning to take?"

Ash looked round the room and held her hands up, helplessly. "There's years of work here – all his notes about the cooling down, and his measurements of the lights in the sphere, his work on crystals… There's so much!"

Ryan was already on his feet and moving things around. "What would a map look like?" he said. "Do you even have books here?"

"Doc," said Graham. "Wouldn't it be easier to go and find the TARDIS? Use that to hop up to the surface and find out what's going on?"

"It might," said the Doctor, "if we knew how to get to it. Er, Quartz," she said, "I don't suppose anyone has mentioned a big blue box to you? Sort of this high…" She reached up her hand over her head. "Well, quite a lot bigger, actually. But blue. You'd know it if you saw it." She opened and closed her fist. "Big flashing light on the top."

"I know what you mean," he said. "Emerald's people have it."

"Emerald," said Yaz. "That name keeps coming up. Who *is* Emerald?"

"Our ruler," said Ash. "Not very fond of my father. Thought he was a troublemaker."

Quartz looked pained. "It's not as simple as that, Ash..."

The Doctor was eyeing Quartz thoughtfully. "It's handy you knew about the TARDIS," she said. "Handy that you know so much of what's going on."

Quartz gave her a glittering smile. "Yes, well, I'm very well connected."

There is something creepy about him, thought Yaz.

"And in point of fact," Quartz went on, "Basalt did tell me his plans for the start of his journey. He left me some of his notes." He glanced at Ash, who had a somewhat hurt expression on her face. "I think he was trying to keep you safe, Ash."

"I suppose so," she said. "Although it was a little late to start thinking about that."

"He knew how hard all this had been on you," Quartz said.

"I believed in him," said Ash, simply. "It wasn't that hard. Not really."

"So where was he going, Quartz?" said the Doctor.

Quartz took out a small crystal, and handed this across to Ash. She ran her fingertips across it. Gentle sounds emerged, as if several people were humming sweetly together, each at a different pitch. "Oh," said Ash. "First he intended to take the White Way."

"That sounds pretty," said Ryan. "The White Way. Nice. Moonlight and stars—"

"They're white-hot lava rapids," said Ash.

"Oh," said Ryan.

"Sounds pretty *and* remarkable!" said the Doctor. "Can't wait!"

Ash looked doubtfully at the Doctor and her friends. "I'm sure everything will be fine."

Four

They took some time to pack some supplies. *"Rope,"* muttered the Doctor. Ash searched the room and found half a dozen lightweight coils, like the one she had used to help them escape their makeshift dungeon. The Doctor sat for a while with her sonic, analysing their composition, and they waited for the night cycle to begin.

As the darkness settled again, they set out. Yaz noticed a strange and beautiful music all around. "What's that sound, Ash?"

"Those are jet-flies," Ash said. "They come out to welcome the night."

"Like crickets," said Yaz.

"'Crickets'," Ash repeated, softly. "That's a pretty word. There aren't so many differences between us, I think. We tell children that jet-flies sing to make their dreams sharp and bright."

Yaz smiled. "That's lovely." *Yes,* she thought, *we've more in common than it seems on the surface.* She liked Ash, and was looking forward to getting to know her better over their journey. "We say, 'sweet dreams'. But the meaning is the same."

Ryan was fascinated by the crystal that Basalt had left. "Does that really hold all his notes? And it's all done by sound?"

"How else would you keep notes so that you could refer back to them?" Quartz said.

"Well..." Ryan looked stuck.

Yaz laughed, wondering how he was going explain paper when there weren't trees. "Go on, Ryan," she said. "Tell him about voice notes."

"Never mind," Ryan said.

"How much of your father's plan is on there?" the Doctor said. "Where was he going beyond the White Way?"

"I'm not sure Basalt entirely knew himself," Quartz said. "His aim, when we last talked, was to find his way around the sphere of the world to the long threads of light we've seen. But nobody has been that way."

Yaz was startled. "What? Never?"

"It's a long way from even our furthest outposts," said Ash.

"But it's only up there," said Yaz.

"That's a long way," said Quartz.

"We have our paths and our patterns," said Ash. "We have everything we need. Why should we go any further?"

"Don't you want to know what's there though?" said Yaz. "I mean, it's right there, in front of you!"

Ash smiled. "You sound like my father."

"Not everyone wants to go on dangerous quests," said the Doctor. "Some people are happy to stay near home. Wouldn't work for me, but there you are. Takes all sorts."

"I'm happy to stay near home," said Ash. "But that doesn't mean I don't want to know the truth about the world."

"Sometimes people have gone adventuring," said Quartz. "For a few days or nights."

"So there's been nothing like this trip of Basalt's in your history?" said the Doctor.

Quartz shook his head. "Nothing."

"That's amazing," said the Doctor. "And now we're following in his footsteps."

Yaz gently touched Ash's arm. "This is very brave of you."

"I just want to find him," Ash said. "Make sure he's safe."

Their first check came not long after they set off. Yaz became aware once again of that strange stillness in the air. She edged up to the Doctor, and saw that she had her sonic screwdriver out, discreetly covered by one hand.

"I don't know what you're thinking," Yaz said, quietly. "But I'm thinking about tsunamis again."

"Yeah, me too," said the Doctor. "I'll have a word with Ash."

"Not Quartz?"

The Doctor glanced back to where Quartz and Graham were walking together. "You know what, Yaz? I'm not a fan of the big fella. Keep an eye on him for me, eh?"

Yaz nodded. She watched the Doctor slip ahead to join Ash and Ryan, and held back to wait for Graham and Quartz.

This meant that they were split into two distinct groups when the pool opened. Yaz heard the same sound that she had before, a sort of crumbling and rumbling and fizzing, and she stopped in her tracks. "Doctor!" she yelled ahead. "It's coming!"

The Doctor, hearing her, pushed Ryan and Ash on ahead, and sprinted off into the gloom. Yaz ran back to Graham.

"What's up?" he said, when she reached him.

"One of those pools is opening! We've got to get back!"

Graham moved surprisingly quickly for a man his age. Quartz could shift too, Yaz noticed. They made for some high ground, a ridge of rock they had just crossed, and looked back to see the jet of water surge upwards, and then flood the narrow piece of low land where they had just been walking.

"Ryan?" yelled Graham. "Where are ya?"

It was all Yaz could do to stop Graham jumping into the boiling water to swim after his grandson. She grabbed his arm. "Graham!" she said, calmly, but clearly; her copper's voice. "He's safe, look! Look!"

Her tone did the trick. Graham stopped pulling at her and he looked across the new river that had opened up. On the far bank, about thirty feet away, safe on another ridge of rock, were Ryan, Ash, and the Doctor. Ryan waved at him.

"Big wave," Graham whispered, and gave Ryan a big wave back.

"See?" Yaz said, authoritatively. "He's fine."

Graham took a deep breath, and relaxed properly. "Yes, yes. Thanks, Yaz love. You're a great kid."

"Eh," she said, gently thumping his arm. "Less of the kid."

"All right, officer! Fair cop!"

They grinned at each other. It could, Yaz thought, have been a lot worse.

She became aware of Quartz standing beside her. He also looked shaken. "That," he said, "was much too close."

"You don't need to tell me that," said Yaz, sharply, earning a puzzled look from Graham. "All right," she said, "how do we get across to join them?"

Quartz was peering over the new lake. "I'm not sure we do," he said. "Look."

Yaz was resisting the urge to bristle back at him, and then she saw the Doctor. The Doctor was pointing at her chest, and at Ash and Ryan, and then pointing behind her. Next she flapped both hands in their direction, as if to send them away: *Shoo!* Then she pointed at them, pointed to her side of the river, and shook her head and arms wildly. Then she started the whole routine again.

"Now I'm not a professional code-breaker," said Graham, "but I think she's telling us that they'll go on." He peered at the Doctor. "*Now* what is she doing?"

The Doctor had her hand over her head. She was opening and closing her fist.

"I think she wants us to find the TARDIS."

"And *now* what?" said Graham.

The Doctor had her hand on her forehead, the fingers splayed out, like the crest on a cockerel. She wiggled her fingers about, and then shook her head, pulling a stern face. Yaz thought she knew what she meant: *Watch out for Quartz.*

Yaz held up both thumbs. The Doctor was now going through her routine from the top. "All right, Doctor. You can stop now. I think we get the message." Yaz flashed her hand over her head and put her thumb up. Then she mimed the crest and put her thumb down. Then she held both thumbs up high. *Message received*. The Doctor lifted her fists above her head and shook them about, like a champion winning a race, mouthing: *Yay!*

"So we should find the TARDIS," said Yaz. "But that's easier said than done. Where would Emerald's guards have taken it, Quartz? Any suggestions?"

"I think I should take you to the City," said Quartz. "To my house."

Yaz thought carefully. They needed to go that way to find the TARDIS, but the Doctor didn't trust Quartz – and yet at the same time she had mimed to Yaz to keep an eye on him. "Won't we stand out?" she said. "I mean, we're not exactly like the rest of you..." She didn't want to be led into a trap. She liked almost everything about travelling with the Doctor, but wasn't a huge fan of the cells and dungeons.

"I know some back routes," said Quartz, with that smooth confidence that Yaz was starting to dislike. "My house is very big."

Good for you, thought Yaz.

He must have caught her look of disapproval. "I simply meant that you can hide there, if necessary."

"Hmm," said Yaz. She was aware of Graham's confusion, but not exactly placed to explain.

"It makes sense," said Graham. "Maybe we can find out where the TARDIS is. Get it back."

Yaz looked across the lake. The others were already on their way. She sighed. "All right," she said. "Let's get to the city. Is it far, Quartz?"

"I'm not sure how you measure either time or distance," he said. "But we will be there shortly."

Yaz didn't like uncertainties, but she followed him as he led the way. Graham hung back to speak to her.

"What have you got against our friend?" he said, nodding ahead at Quartz's glittering back.

"The Doctor didn't like him."

"Oh, he's a bit of a show-off, yes, but he's all right. Besides, we're stuck, aren't we? There's no-one else here who can help us."

Yaz sighed. He was right; and she didn't like that one bit.

"Right," said the Doctor, looking up at the ridge of rock rising steadily ahead of them. "The only way is up." She stopped. "Hey, that's quite catchy."

"Someone's done that song already, Doctor," said Ryan, helpfully.

"Yeah? Oh well, never mind." She turned to Ash. "How far to the White Way?"

"Not far now. Over these ridges, then down into the valley."

"Lava rapids here we come," said Ryan. "A bit intrepid, your dad, wasn't he?"

"*Isn't* he," said Ash, pointedly. "He *is* intrepid."

"Yes, of course, sorry, Ash. I didn't mean—"

"It's all right, Ryan." Ash sighed. "I'm worrying about where we go after that. His notes don't tell me much more…"

Ryan patted her arm. "The Doctor will work it out."

They walked on. Ash led the party, with Ryan next, and the Doctor at the rear, ready in case anyone lost their footing. They soon crossed the rocky ridge, and, to Ryan's relief, there was a smooth path leading down the other side. They could hear the crashing of a river in the distance.

As they walked down the valley, Ryan quizzed the Doctor. "Why didn't you want the others to try and join us?"

"Well," she said, "for one thing, that new river looked pretty dangerous. For another – I'm hoping they'll go back to the City and find out what's going on there. Maybe even find the TARDIS." She sighed.

"But?" said Ryan.

"How did you guess there was something else on my mind?" the Doctor said.

"You had one of your faces. Your 'I've-got-something-else-on-my-mind' face."

"I'm starting to wonder how many faces this body has got."

"They're all nice faces," Ryan said, gallantly.

"Ooh, you charmer!"

"I try! So – what's the matter?"

"I'm not too sure about Quartz. I'd rather he was here where I could keep an eye on him."

Ryan frowned. "Will Yaz and Graham be all right?"

"I'm hoping they can give him the slip… Anyway, those two can look after themselves," said the Doctor. Ryan walked on, trying not to worry. He wouldn't like to get on the wrong side of Yaz in a dark alley and as for his granddad – well, he'd lasted this long more or less intact, hadn't he? And Yaz would keep an eye on him, Ryan consoled himself.

As the dark began to lift, they came to the head of the rapids.

"Look around," Ash said. "We're looking for a boat. A coracle."

They hunted around. The Doctor found it, calling to the others to help her carry it. The boat was bowl-shaped, hollowed and smoothed from stone, with oars made from what Ryan, touching one, realised was a kind of tough fibre, much thicker than whatever Ash's people used to make their ropes. He wondered what kind of plant it came from.

"Are there always boats here, Ash?" the Doctor said.

"People come this way sometimes, on their way round the sphere," Ash said. "There are usually several boats. My father must have taken the others." She smiled. "That's good news."

"Have you been here before?" Ryan said.

"Yes, with my father."

Ryan looked out at the crashing white waves. *It's not water*, he thought.

"What do you think, Ryan?" said the Doctor. "Shall we give it a go?"

"As long as Ash steers," said Ryan. "Hey, Ash, how many times have you done this?"

"Once," said Ash.

"Oh. Well. Better than nothing, I suppose."

"I mean *this* once," Ash said.

The Doctor laughed out loud. "Oh, Ash! You're very dry!"

"I'm made of rock," she said, her eyes gleaming.

They clambered into the boat, and paddled out slowly. Ash seemed to know what she was doing, Ryan thought – which was more than he felt he could say for himself. "Doctor," he murmured, "I'm not sure I'm cut out for this—"

"Give it a go," she said. "Ash will be doing the bulk of the work. We're just here to help push the boat forwards."

And then they were off, caught in the flow of the white-hot lava. "Oh my *days*!" shouted Ryan, as the world whipped past. "Oh *man*!"

They sped along. Ryan whooped out loud with delight, and the Doctor whooped at least as much, if not more. Then, from the corner of his eye, Ryan saw huge domed shapes rise up from the magma. Ash was doing a good job of dodging between them, but Ryan's oar brushed against one. It came out sticky. He was about to reach out to touch, when he heard Ash's voice, shouting out above the roar of the rocks. "Jellyfish!" she cried. "Don't touch them! They give a nasty sting!"

Ryan pulled his hand back hastily. Ash kept the boat dodging through the creatures. Then something else rose out of the lava. Ryan had an impression of bulk, and teeth, and a roaring, scraping sound.

"Lavashark!" cried Ash.

"What should I do?" yelled Ryan, then remembered something about bopping them on the nose to drive sharks away. He lifted up his oar and whacked it, hard.

"Don't do that!" yelled Ash. "You'll make it mad!"

Sure enough, the beast lunged up, and for a moment Ryan thought he was going to lose the oar to its maw. Then the shark pulled back. Ryan breathed a sigh of relief, and then realised that the beast was only backing up to come back and hammer the side of their little boat. They rocked about, perilously. "Ash!" Ryan cried. "It's still there!"

"Don't worry, Ryan, I'm on it!" shouted the Doctor. She pushed her oar down beneath the surface, and flipped up one of the jellyfish onto its flat surface. "Here," she said. "Catch this!" She lobbed the jellyfish up into the air. Ryan stuck up his oar, and, with a flick of the wrist, sent it flying to land flat on the shark's nose. It roared with rage, and slunk away beneath the surface.

"Gotcha!" Ryan yelled.

"Nice job," the Doctor shouted back at him. "Two thousand bonus points!"

Ryan laughed. She was right. It *was* like a game, but he was here, for real, right in the thick of things. Turned out those video games had been good for something after all. His reflexes were better than he thought they were. *I can do this*, Ryan thought. *Gran, I can do this…*

And then, suddenly, the river widened out, and its course became smooth.

They were through the White Way.

Gently, Ash steered the little boat towards the shore. The Doctor and Ryan clambered out, and then they both fell onto the bank, helpless with laughter.

"Doctor," said Ryan. "That was *brilliant!*"

"It was though, wasn't it?"

"I wish we could go round again!"

"Me too!"

They lay on their backs, catching their breath. Ash sat down beside them, watching them with steady, curious eyes.

"Promise me one thing, though, Doctor," said Ryan.

"What?" the Doctor said.

"Never leave me alone with a lavashark."

The Doctor's face crinkled with laughter. "Cross my hearts."

Far, far away, Yasmin and Graham stood side by side and looked again at the Diamond City.

"Wow," said Graham. "It really is a sight for sore eyes!"

Yaz was thinking of an experiment she had done as a kid. You tipped a pile of chemicals into a little plastic jar, and then crystals grew. It had seemed magical, although the teacher had been at pains to explain the process behind it. She had never imagined she had would see the same thing the size of a city. Was that how it had been built? Had they grown crystals in the same way, she wondered, but on a much larger scale? And then they fashioned them into homes, halls, streets, and walkways, and decorated them with precious stones and colourful rocks, until the whole place gleamed and shone...

Quartz was smiling at the sight. For a brief moment, Yaz felt sympathy with him, a fellow feeling. He had shown her his home, and wanted her to be impressed – and she had been, very impressed. She imagined leading him up one of the hills around Sheffield, looking down on its slate grey buildings and the rough grass that grew doggedly whenever it had the chance. She loved her city, and she would want a stranger to admire it. She wondered what Quartz would think of it; how alien it would seem to him, under the big Yorkshire sky.

Quartz sighed and pointed upwards. "Look."

Yaz looked up. High above them, in the dark of the roof of the world, at the far side of the sphere, she saw faint smears. "Those shooting stars again," said Graham.

"Like the Milky Way," said Yaz.

"Stars, but on the inside," said Graham. "I can't get my head around this."

"I'm not sure I understand what you mean when you say 'stars'," said Quartz.

"Lights up in the sky," said Graham. "Hang on, that won't make any sense, will it?"

"Basalt used to talk about what the surface of a world must be like," said Quartz. "Most alarming. A sphere outside our own sphere. Nothing above…" He shuddered. "How you feel safe, crawling along like that I do not know. But, no, these aren't the kind of lights in the sky that you must be used to. This is something far more worrying. This is what Basalt was trying to tell people."

"Cracks," said Yaz. "Cracks in the sphere, right above your City."

"Like being inside an egg shell," said Graham.

"But seeing those," said Yaz, gesturing upwards, "and knowing that there are pools opening – people aren't connecting the two?"

"People won't admit it," said Quartz. "They'd rather pretend that they're new streams of silver, or something like that."

"And nobody's been to have a look?" said Graham.

"It's like Ash said, we stay close together. If Basalt has got all the way there, he hasn't sent a message back."

"And, in the meantime, everyone's denying the evidence of their own eyes," said Graham. "Bad idea."

"And saying anything out loud can get people into trouble." Quartz sighed, deeply. "Come on," he said. "We can be seen easily here, and Emerald has many ways of watching people as they approach her city."

Reluctantly, they turned their back on the shining sight, and followed Quartz.

"I wish Ryan had been here to see that," said Graham, with a sigh.

"The Doctor will be back as soon as she's found out what's going on," Yaz said, robustly.

"But how long will that be?" said Graham. "I mean, how long does it take to travel from one side of this sphere to the other? Do you have any idea? Because I don't."

"Try not to make too much noise," said Quartz, politely. "We're trying to move in secret, after all."

He led them on until the path came to a dead end in front of a sheer wall of pale yellow stone. Yaz was suddenly on alert. Was this some kind of trap? Had Quartz brought them here so that they could be captured? She glanced around quickly. There was no way out other than the way they had come.

Quartz, as if guessing her thoughts, gave a sly smile. Then he put his hand up to the smooth face of the stone, and pushed, very hard. The rock rolled back.

"Blimey," said Graham. "A proper secret tunnel. What's that place called... You know, Yaz, with the stones and the rocks and those screechy little fellas? In that film of Ryan's."

Yaz thought about this for a while. "Do you mean the Mines of Moria?"

Graham snapped his fingers. "That's it! Mines of Moria." His face fell, and Yaz knew he was worrying about Ryan. But there was no time – Quartz gestured to them to follow, and they went through the door and into the dark.

Not far from the river, where the Doctor and her friends had landed, there was another path, narrow and not as well kept as others they had taken. Ash hesitated by this, but then nodded, and led Ryan and the Doctor that way.

"Where did your father say he was going next?" the Doctor said.

"That's the problem," Ash admitted. "He doesn't mention a route after this. But there's only one way my people go after the White Way, and that's towards the Grey Forest."

"Grey Forest," said Ryan. "I'm not going to make any guesses this time. What's it like in there?"

"We don't go in," Ash said. "If people go this way, they go round."

"Any particular reason why?" said Ryan.

"Why go to the trouble of hacking through a forest when there's a perfectly good route through open ground around it?" she said.

"Fair enough," said Ryan, although he couldn't help wondering whether there was a *quicker* way if you went through…

The land they were passing through was getting wilder, with strange shrubs and bushes. They were far from the rocky plain near where the TARDIS had landed, and this land was clearly much more fecund than the dry cracked land where the lava sea had been. They came over another ridge, and he saw the dark expanse of the forest up ahead. "Not far," said Ash.

The shrubs and bushes got thicker, and sometimes there were even bright specks of flowers. There was wildlife too; flittering insects with gem-like eyes, and small creatures that skittered away when you walked past. Nothing big, Ryan thought with relief, although the ruby rats were a problem. The thing was, they got *everywhere*… You sat down, and realised there was one nibbling at your finger. You jumped up, and the thing had already found its way down to scratch at your boots… And their *teeth*… So sharp! It made sense, he thought, if they were made of precious stones. He just didn't want to experiment how sharp using one of his fingers.

"These things," he said, waving his hand to shoo another one away, "will be the death of me."

Ash's eyes opened wide. Ryan was starting to get the hang of reading her expressions now. It hadn't been easy, at first, but as you spent more time with her, you realised that what seemed to be a solid wall of, well, *rock*, was actually really supple. She picked up the rat that he'd shaken off, cupping it between her hands, and carried it away a little distance before setting it free. When she came back, she still had that expression of concern.

"I sincerely hope they won't cause your death, Ryan," she said. "They're certainly not dangerous for us, although I do understand that your carapaces are not quite…" She stopped for a moment, as if trying to think of a way to express herself politely. "Not quite as *hardy*."

"Carapace?" Ryan said, puzzled. "Oh! Skin! Nah, not quite as hardy, I suppose." He shook his leg, sending yet another ruby rat dashing into the foliage. "It's OK. That's just an expression. Be good to get past this lot of them, though."

The Doctor, who had been poking around a few feet away, looked up. "Don't you like them, Ryan? I was thinking of bringing one with us."

He looked at her. "You what?"

"As a pet, you know?" She was peering down at the ground, and he realised with a sinking heart that she was trying to find one of the beasts. "Or, I should say, so I can make a proper study of them…"

"Doctor," he said, "they've got teeth."

"Well, so have you," she said. "And I've never held that against you. Oh, hang on! There's one!" She went dashing off, into the undergrowth, like Alice after the white rabbit. "Hey," she cried. "Come back!"

"Doctor!" Ryan yelled. "Don't just run off!" He huffed. "Honestly, sometimes it's like following a toddler around …"

Beside him, Ash was making an odd sound, like pebbles sliding together at the start of an avalanche. Ryan turned to her in concern, and then realised she was laughing.

"She reminds me of my father," Ash said. "Always chasing a new idea."

Ryan nodded his understanding. He thought of his gran; always at the front, ready for adventure, ready to have a go. *I'm trying, Gran*, he thought. *Trying to give things a go.*

The Doctor reappeared. "It got away. Never mind, plenty more where that came from. And look – I found something interesting."

She came towards them, and Ryan and Ash leaned in to see what she was carrying. For a moment, Ryan thought she had found a laptop – it was about the same size, and a steely grey colour – and then he realised this was daft. It couldn't be, and, besides, the thing was made of stone.

"I feel like Moses," the Doctor said, holding the stone tablet up. "Nice man, bit beardy."

"Doctor," said Ryan, gently reminding her of the task at hand, "what is it?"

"Well, I know a message when I see one," the Doctor said. She placed the stone tablet on the ground. "Ash – am I right?"

Ryan knelt down to get a better look. He couldn't see a message, only flecks of mica. He reached out to clear some of it away, but the Doctor stopped him. "Let Ash look."

Ash studied the stone and gasped out loud.

"I'm right, aren't I?" said the Doctor.

"Yes," Ash said. "This is my father's name, here…" She pointed to some of the flecks. Ryan was glad he hadn't tried to brush any of it off.

"What did he say?" The Doctor's voice was quiet, but urgent.

Ash looked up, wretchedly. "I don't know," she said. "He's used some kind of code."

"Doesn't make things easy, your dad, does he?" said Ryan.

The Doctor rubbed her hands together in glee. "I love a good code."

Five

Ryan sat, patiently, while Ash and the Doctor pored over the stone. Not far, huge and looming and whispering, stood the fringes of the forest, daring them to enter.

Ryan stood up and walked closer to look at some of the plants. He would be the first to admit that he was hardly what you could call a gardener, but these were like nothing he had ever seen. First his eye fell on some low thick bushes at the very edge of the forest. They were not quite the right colour, for one thing; not green, but instead they had a yellowish hue, fading to dark brown closer to the ground. When he looked closely, he saw that the bushes weren't formed from stems and leaves, but from thick brown veins that looked like they'd be squishy to touch, and which fanned out into yellow plate-sized circles. Behind the bushes were taller plants – more like trees – which glowed, faintly, pale pink, like a lamp behind frosted glass. Between the trees and the buses were long silver trailing plants, thin as cobwebs, and these too shone, like strings of fairy lights on a Christmas tree. Ryan reached out to touch one of them. He had expected something gossamer light. Instead it was tough, and wiry. He thought of the ropes that Ash had handed round.

"Doctor," he called back over to her. "Come and have a look at all this."

The Doctor came to join him. She ran her sonic screwdriver over one of the nearest plants. She was particularly interested in the wiry fibres that he showed her. "*Rope*," she muttered. "*Rope*."

"Are these kinda like… mushrooms?"

"Great guess, Ryan. Yep, these are fungi of some sort." She stood rapt for a while, staring into the depths of the forest. "That's amazing."

Ryan nodded. It *was* amazing, although the overall effect was just this side of terrifying, and he had a very strong suspicion about which way they were heading once Ash had got to grips with her father's code. Again, he found himself missing Graham and Yaz. He wondered where they were, and what they were doing; whether they were seeing sights as weird and wonderful as this, and whether they were all right. Yaz, he thought, would be loving this whole business; Graham would be loving it too, although at a slightly slower pace. As for Ryan himself… He reached out to touch one of the wiry trailing plants. A smile crept across his face. Yes, he thought, he was loving all this as well.

"How's it going, Ash?" said the Doctor.

Ash looked up from her task. "Slow," she admitted. "He taught me most of his codes – I took a lot of his notes for him. But this isn't one I've seen before."

"Did he always write in code?" said Ryan.

"Almost always," said Ash.

"He'd have to," said the Doctor. "If people found out what he was planning, he would be in trouble."

"I really thought he'd taught me all the main ones he used," Ash said. "It seems not." She sounded hurt by this, as if this meant that he had decided not to trust her. Ryan didn't believe that was the case. He knew what protective adults looked like.

"You'll do it," the Doctor said, placing one hand gently upon Ash's shoulder. "I don't think he didn't trust you with his secrets, you know. I think he knew he could trust you to crack his most difficult code."

Ash smiled. That idea seemed to console her considerably, and she and the Doctor went back to the task with renewed enthusiasm. Ryan wandered towards the edge of the forest. He peered inside at the thick tangle of interwoven plants. If this was their route (and he was sure it would be) then how would they get through? Could the Doctor's sonic clear a path? He wasn't sure there was enough power, although the sonic did seem able to pull off all sorts of tricks. But he suspected that hacking through this spooky place was going to involve muscle and hard work. He leaned inwards, and listened, closely. In the distance, far under this strange canopy, he heard the swish of some unknown, alien life; the call of some weird creature. Things lived in there. Things never seen before by human eyes; strange and unknown life, and all in danger from the threat that lay hanging over this world. There *must* be some way in and through, he thought. This incredible place couldn't be lost for ever...

"Ryan!" called the Doctor. "We think we've cracked it!"

Ryan hurried back to them. Ash lay the stone tablet on the ground for them to see. As she spoke, she pointed at various sections of the mica runes. "This describes their route so far. We know that. They came along the White Way, just like us." She laughed. "He took the time to take some samples from the jellyfish, and he's left notes about the composition of a possible antidote for their sting. That is *exactly* like him. A hundred different projects, all at once."

The Doctor smiled. "Always the scientist. I do like your dad."

"This section explains where they're going next," Ash said.

"It's into the forest, isn't it?" said Ryan.

Ash looked up and blinked. "How did you guess that?"

"Well, look at it," Ryan said. "Huge, shady, threatening. Made of mushrooms. Where else was it going to be?"

The Doctor nudged him. "Cheer up," she said. "It's like Mirkwood!"

"Doctor," Ryan said. "Mirkwood was full of giant spiders and an evil wizard."

"Oh yeah," she said. "I always forget that bit. I only ever remember the Elves." She turned back to Ash. "Does your father give a clue about the way through, Ash?"

Ash shook her head. "If he and his people went deep into the forest, they've gone further than any of us ever have. We go round to reach our settlements." She pondered the tablet again. A couple of ruby rats wriggled through and started gnawing at the stone. Absently, she brushed them away. "But these seem to be directions. We skirt the edge of the forest a little further, and then there's a way through the undergrowth, almost a path…" She looked up. "What do you think, Doctor?"

"What do I think? I think we should go take a look, of course."

They walked on. Beside them the forest glowed and whispered, as if beckoning: *Come inside… Come and see what enchantments lie within…*

They followed Basalt's directions and, as he had promised, they soon came to a place where the forest thinned slightly, allowing people to enter, if they walked single file. On the threshold was another stone tablet. Ash got to work at once. "They certainly intended to enter the forest here," she said, at last. "What this can't tell us is how far they got."

"Only one way to find out," the Doctor said. She led the way forwards, and they dived into the forest.

The tunnels were low, and both Yaz and Graham had to stoop to be able to carry on walking. What little light there was came from crystals set in the wall here and there, like lanterns in a mediaeval castle.

"Like those tunnels in Gaul," whispered Graham. "They had them in Rome, too. Mary Berry said so."

"Mary Beard," Yaz reminded him.

"That's what I said. Isn't it?"

Yaz smiled in the half-light. She was glad of Graham's solid presence. Yaz could take care of herself – but it was nice to know that others cared enough to be looking out for you. And everyone needed a helping hand every so often.

"Anyway," Graham said, "the catacombs in Rome were built so that the Christians could hide away from the authorities." He called ahead. "Quartz? Who made these tunnels? What are they for?"

Quartz, who had been leading the way, hung back for a moment until they caught up. "We're a close-knit family here," he said. "And there was a time – not so long ago – when we were forbidden to leave the City for more a night. But there are always adventurers, even here…"

"Like Basalt," said Yaz.

"Like Basalt. Some people wanted to travel more freely. They had good reasons too – there were more of us than ever, and not enough food. So they dug these passages to be able to meet each other, and make plans, and then they built tunnels that ran beyond the City walls. After a while, the need for more resources became acute, and the laws were relaxed, and now we can travel beyond the City for great distances. As long as there's a good reason – to forage, or hunt, or mine."

"What about if you just want to go for a wander?" said Graham. "You know, a bit of a holiday? Get away from it all."

Quartz gave a wry smile. "That isn't generally allowed."

"So Basalt's journey…?" said Yaz.

"He didn't have permission," said Quartz. "Quite the contrary, I should imagine, if anyone had heard about it before he left."

"Permission!" said Graham. "What is this? School?"

Yaz pondered what Quartz had said. A civilisation so enclosed, so close-knit, that even going a day away from the City had once been forbidden. No wonder Basalt's ideas had caused so much trouble. For the first time, she had an inkling of what it might mean to these people to see aliens amongst them; to be confronted with the truth of life beyond the safe small sphere of their world.

At length, they came down a short tunnel and were stopped by a rock rolled into place, blocking the way through. "My home is behind this," said Quartz. Yaz and Graham helped him move the rock aside: it was a kind of pumice and deceptively light. Quartz led them into a wide hall, carved from crystal, which glowed gently from within.

"Wow," murmured Graham. "How the other half lives."

"Welcome!" Quartz said. He led them further inside, along richly glowing passageways, bringing them at last to a large room that shimmered with ever-changing light. "Make yourself comfortable," he said, gesturing round. "I have a few things to see to, and then we can talk about our next move."

He left through another door. Yaz and Graham looked at each other in amazement.

"What a place," said Graham. "Look at that light show!"

Yaz nodded. It was like being inside a big church when the sun shone through the stained glass, painting the walls with colour. Only here the colours shifted, and came from the walls themselves. "It's gorgeous, I guess."

"You guess?" Graham frowned. "What's the matter?"

"I'm still not sure about Quartz. Who do you know with a secret passage leading straight to their house?"

"We don't know much about these people, do we? Maybe they *all* have secret passages leading straight to their house. From what he said half of them were running around them at one point."

Yaz laughed. "Not very secret, then!"

"Yeah, you'd always be bumping into the neighbours. 'Oh, sorry, I was just down here in this secret passage, didn't mean to disturb you…'"

Yaz felt cheered as always by Graham's chatter, as was probably his intention. The colours on the wall seemed warmer now. She sat down in a huge chair, carved from a single slab of dark grey slate, and tried to get comfortable. Graham too was having the same problem.

"What this place needs is more cushions," he said.

Quartz returned then, carrying a tray with stone plates which he placed on a marble table. "I don't know whether you can eat or drink any of this," he said. "But I try to be hospitable…"

Yaz and Graham peered at his offering: small slices of various coloured substance that could be brown bread, or cheddar cheese, or who knew what.

"It looks nice," said Yaz, doubtfully.

"Oh, I'll go first," Graham said. He took a bite from one of the small slices laid out. "Tastes fine. Tastes… mushroomy."

Yaz gave it a couple of minutes, and then, when Graham didn't keel over, took the risk herself. He was right. Everything was fine – nice, even. She realised how hungry she was, and sampled everything that Quartz had brought. Graham turned out to have a bottle of water stashed on him, which they shared, taking small sips to conserve the supply.

A bell rang – no, more like wind-chimes clattering persistently. Yaz jumped up from her chair. "Is there someone here? I thought we were safe—"

Quartz raised his hands to placate her. "It's all right. There's nothing to worry about. I've asked a few friends to come and join us."

"A few *friends*?" Yaz said, but Quartz was already out of the door. She turned to Graham. "Do you think we can get away? Did you see another way out?"

"I don't think we've got time to try!" Graham sighed. "Looks like we're meeting these friends, then. Well, we'll see what they have to say."

Quartz came back in, a handful of figures following. Yaz's first impression was of a dazzling array of crystals and gems, of precious stones and shimmering colours. It took her a moment to see faces, eyes, mouths – people. There was a short silence as the humans stared at the rock-people, and the rock-people stared back.

"Yasmin, Graham – these are my friends," said Quartz. "Friends of mine, and friends of Basalt. We really do want to help you, however we can."

The journey through the forest was an unsettling experience. Everything looked similar to something from Earth – the bushes, the trees, the trailing plants, the bright flowers – but as you got closer, they were all so very different that Ryan would almost feel thrown off-balance, as if someone had performed a conjuring trick before his eyes. Then there were the odd noises – chirrups and creaks, nothing like birdsong or any insect he had heard.

The scents of the forest were different too – dry, and stuffy. Mouldering. Progress was slow. In places the path was overgrown, and Ash would have to stop and ponder the best way. Sometimes the Doctor would stop too, and hold up the sonic screwdriver, and frown, and suggest a course correction, or nod, and they would carry on.

"What are you doing, Doctor?" Ryan asked, on one of these occasions.

"We're heading for those cracks we saw in the sphere, yeah?" she said. "We can't see them under all this," she gestured around the forest, "but I can still navigate us, roughly."

"Like GPS," he said.

"Sort of. Geo-Positioning Sonic. And there's something else…"

"What else?" said Ryan.

She shoved the screwdriver away. "I'm not sure yet. Don't worry."

Every so often, to their excitement, they came across another of Basalt's stone tablets, showing they were on the right lines, and would stop for a while so to decipher his latest message. Ash in particular was getting adept at the task, more and more familiar with the code he was using, but it still took her some effort. At least it was a break from walking. As she worked on one of these, Ryan posed the question currently uppermost in his mind.

"Doctor, how long is this walk gonna take?"

The Doctor shook her head. "If we had the TARDIS, we'd be up on the surface in a jiffy. But without? Who knows?" She looked at him thoughtfully. "Graham and

Yaz will be fine, you know. He'll look out for her; she'll look out for him."

"I know, I know…"

"But you're still worried?

"Yeah, of course. But there's something else…"

"What is it?"

"I'm starving." Ryan grinned. "And I need your advice on the only thing we've got on the menu."

"What?" said the Doctor.

He threw his arms out wide. "Mushrooms!"

Her face crinkled up. "Oh yeah! Are you all right with mushrooms?"

"Well, I like a fry-up as much as the next guy, but if I know anything about the great outdoors, it's that you don't help yourself to any mushrooms you find lying around the place."

"Absolutely not," said the Doctor. "The last thing you should do is try mushrooms without knowing what they are. Double that for alien mushrooms. *Triple* that for alien mushrooms."

She pulled out her sonic screwdriver and started breaking small pieces of the various plants to hand, testing them one by one. "Not that. Not that. Ooh, dear, no, *definitely* not that…" After a little while, she settled on one. "This will be fine," she said. "Actually, this will be good for you. Should help keep stress levels down." She frowned. "This is the thing with wiping out flora and fauna. You never know which one is going to contain a cure for some disease. You know, there was a flower that only grew high up on one mountainside on Eltemalisia Magna which turned out to contain a compound that could cure Flugel's Ague, and they were going to flatten the mountain – can't remember why now, it's usually a road, isn't it? Anyway, it was a particularly nice little flower, it had pale blue spiky petals with white bits and a really nice scent that would go *foof* in your face when the temperature was right, like a little spray of fancy perfume. It was lovely! I mean, even if it hadn't contained the cure for Flugel's Ague, there still wouldn't be any excuse to go around pulverising a mountain—"

"Doctor," Ryan said, plaintively. "I'm *starving*."

"Oh yeah. Sorry. It really is a nice flower though." She nibbled at the piece of fungus that she had broken off, and then handed him the rest.

Ryan peered down. It looked all right – like a slice of an ordinary, if oversized, Earth mushroom. He popped the piece in his mouth, ready to spit it out again, and then realised it tasted nice. "Hey," he said. "That's all right, isn't it? All it needs is a couple of fried eggs, some tomatoes, and a pile of bacon." He nibbled at the mushrooms and watched as the Doctor foraged further, coming back with a stack of big leaves. She split the leaves in two, and sap oozed out. "We can drink this," she said. "Until we find water."

Ash came to join them. She was looking cheerful: they were on the right path, and simply had to continue the way they were going. She saw what they were eating, and smiled.

"Oh," she said. "I wondered what you'd eat. I even wondered if you *did* eat."

"Believe me," said Ryan, fervently, "we eat."

"Those are nice," Ash said. "I like them for breakfast, sizzling in the pan with jet cakes and hot sauce."

Ryan groaned. "I don't know what any of that is, but just hearing you say that is making me hungrier."

The Doctor gave her brilliant smile. "Ryan, I promise you – when we've saved this world, you'll have the fry-up of your life."

Yaz had not felt under this much scrutiny since the whole of Year Ten had been in trouble for mucking about on their trip to Haworth. Half-a-dozen strange faces were staring at her, more alarming than any teacher-led court martial. One of this lot, for example, she was sure, had more than two eyes; another had eyes that as yet had not blinked. Yet another was bright white, its whole body seeming to shine from within with an almost blinding light, flecked through with silver and grey. Most of them had strange and beautiful formations, like Quartz's crown, perhaps around their wrists, or ridges across their back or shoulders. They all looked so different, Yaz thought, and yet they were clearly all of the same species.

At last, one of them, with a silvery veins running across its face, spoke. "What... what *are* you?"

Graham, to his credit, didn't seem in the least bit fazed. "We're human beings," he said, proudly. "From the planet Earth. We're friendly and we're very nice!" He turned to Yaz, suddenly self-conscious. "Is there some sort of official way of doing this?"

"Why are you asking me?"

"Well, you're a copper, ain't ya? Don't you do training for this kind of things? You know, official stuff?"

"I promise you, they didn't cover 'meeting and greeting aliens' in copper school." Yaz relented slightly. "I thought what you said was cool."

Graham looked genuinely pleased. "Oh, thanks! I tried!"

"Ooman beengs?" said the silver-veined person.

Graham smiled. "That's right! More or less. Close enough!"

"This one is Graham," Quartz said, helpfully. "And this one is Yaz. Those are their names."

The aliens turned to each other and murmured to each other for a while, casting furtive glances every so often at the strange visitors. Yaz watched them closely. There was confusion, alarm, some fear – and here and there she thought she caught something of that particular sense of wonder which she associated with her travels with the Doctor, as if the whole universe had suddenly been proven to be more varied and interesting and alarming than she had ever before imagined possible.

Eventually, the silvered person spoke again. "Yes, but… what *are* you?"

Graham looked stumped, but gamely tried again. "I guess – well, we're aliens I suppose, aren't we?"

"We're not from this planet," Yaz tried, then wondered whether they had any idea, really, of what a planet was. What had Basalt said? "Beyond your home," she said, "you come to the surface—"

"Just as Basalt claimed," Quartz said. "All of you, you heard him speak many times. You know what he always said. That we lived in a hollow, and beyond that was thick rock, and beyond that, the surface of a sphere of which we are the centre. You believed him, didn't you?"

"Yes, I believed him," said the unblinking one. He was dark blue, with paler swirls all over him, like lapis lazuli. "But he never said anything about – well." He stared fiercely at the humans. "Things like this!"

One of the others had moved closer to Graham. She reached out a rocky fingertip and, tentatively, touched his skin. "Oh!" she cried. "It's *soft*!"

"Thank you," said Graham. "I don't think I'd sell many cosmetics, but it's always nice to get a compliment."

She poked him again. "It's *squishy*!"

"I'm a 'he' rather than an 'it', actually," Graham said. "Oh, you mean my skin."

"You're right," said Yaz. "We're not made from rock like you. We're something else."

"Are you from the surface?" asked another one, a quiet one sitting near the back, beautiful onyx with white swirls across his arms and chest.

"So many questions!" said Quartz. "I asked you here because we need your help—"

"Wait, Quartz," said the silver-veined one, lifting his hand. "I'd like an answer to that. Basalt said that we were inside a great sphere with a surface. Are these people from that surface, high above us?"

Graham opened his mouth to answer, but Yaz shook her head and he stopped. She had a sudden feeling that they were on the edge of something very significant, that what they said now might have a dramatic effect on these people. She wanted them to choose their words carefully. "No," she said. "We're not from the surface."

The silver-veined one pressed on. "And you're not from a part of this world – this 'sphere', our own sphere – that we have not yet discovered?"

There were some murmurs around the group; clearly they had seen where their friend was going with this too. "No," said Yaz. "We're not from this world at all."

The muttering was getting more heated.

"When you reach the surface of this world," Yaz said, "you look out into a vast empty space. If you travel through that space – and you can travel through it, with the right tools and machines – you eventually come to other worlds. We're from one of those. Our friend, the Doctor, is from another, and there are more and more worlds, oh countless, and countless different people, all looking different and doing things differently! It's *so* amazing—"

She had thought that was she conveying some of her excitement, her enthusiasm, for what her life with the Doctor had shown her, had given her. She wasn't really prepared for the reaction she received. The dark blue one, Lapis Lazuli, jumped to his feet.

"Quartz," he said, angrily. "I can't believe you've brought us here to listen to this—"

"It all seems to be true," said Quartz, mildly. Yaz was grudgingly impressed at his calm.

"No! It's lies!" said the silver-veined one.

"It's worse than that," said Lapis Lazuli. "It's heresy."

A heated argument followed; some denying what they could see; others demanding more proof; one or two trying to calm the rest, to no avail. At the back, the onyx one sat quietly, and, catching Yaz's eye, smiled at her. At length, Lapis Lazuli left, angrily, and the others followed shortly after. Last to go was the onyx one, who looked back at Graham and Yaz, and smiled again, and nodded.

At last, Yaz and Graham were alone, with Quartz.

"Right then!" said Graham. "I think that went well!"

Six

Quartz stood looking over at the door through which all his friends had left. He seemed to be at a loss as to what to do next. He shook his head. "I'll speak to them all again," he said. "Perhaps one-by-one... That might make things easier. Some of them were more sympathetic than others, I thought... But it's a huge shock." He stared at his guests again and shook his head. "You're so..."

"We know," said Yaz. "Alien."

"We understand," said Graham.

Yaz and Graham took the chance to rest. Quartz showed them to a pleasant side chamber where beds had been laid out for them.

"Look, Graham," said Yaz, "cushions."

He lifted one and pretended to throw it at her. "Hey, I wonder what these are made out of. Can't be wool or anything like that, can it? Or do you think they have sapphire-sheep and lava-goats?"

"I'd love to see a lava-goat," said Yaz.

"I'm not so sure myself," said Graham.

Yaz ran her hand across the cushions, and the covers on the bed. They had a fibrous feel, like the rope they had used, but more finely woven. "Could be the fleece of a lava-goat, for all we know," she said. "Or the hide of a ruby rat, or mushrooms… Oh, this place is so strange – and creepy! I miss the sunlight, and the fresh air… I feel like we've been stuck indoors forever. Even when we're outside, it just doesn't feel right! And I wish – I *really* wish – that we could contact the Doctor."

Graham put a comforting hand on her shoulder. "It won't be long. You know what the Doctor's like. She always finds a way. Let's have a bit of kip, eh? Things always seem better in the morning."

Yaz lay down on the bed. She didn't think she would be able to rest in this strange room, beneath strange blankets, but all the walking they had done caught up with her, and soon she was soon sleeping deeply. She woke, suddenly, to the realisation that somebody was shaking her. She opened her eyes to find Quartz looming over her. She shrank back – from his bulk, his weight, his sheer and overwhelming difference.

"Don't be afraid," he said. His voice was gentle, but urgent. "But you must get up now – both of you."

"What's going on?" Yaz said. She got up and went to the other bed to shake Graham awake.

"I've had a message from a friend," Quartz said. "He was here last night. It seems that another one of the people you met last night took fright at the sight of you. Didn't like what you were saying. Reported you for heresy."

"Who was it?" said Graham.

"I bet I can guess," said Yaz. "The blue one, or the silvery one."

"It doesn't matter," said Quartz. "What matters is that you and I still have friends, and that they've warned me that the Greenwatch is coming."

Graham, who had been rubbing his eyes, snapped awake. "What?"

"I can get you away, I think," Quartz said. "But we have to leave now."

"Where will we go?" said Yaz.

"Back to the tunnels first," said Quartz.

"And then?" said Graham.

Quartz hesitated. "I'm not sure. Maybe… Maybe back to Basalt's study."

"That's a long way," said Graham.

"Do the tunnels go that far?" said Yaz.

"No…" Quartz admitted. "But we'll think of something."

Yaz and Graham, both wide awake now, followed Quartz as he raced them through his home, and back out through the secret door into the tunnels. He was going at a very fast pace. Yaz, struggling to keep up, thought that the passages were much darker than she remembered from their earlier journey.

"He's in a hurry," said Graham. He was a little out of breath.

"Can you run?" said Yaz.

"Yes, but—"

"Come on then!" Yaz started to jog off, anxious about losing Quartz, but conscious of Graham, straggling behind her. She was aware, as she chased after Quartz, of dark tunnels opening every so often on either side, leading – where? She hadn't the faintest idea. She saw a purplish gleam ahead – Quartz's crest, she thought – but it was disappearing quickly into the distance. She looked back over her shoulder for Graham, who was coming as quickly as he could. Yaz looked ahead.

"Wait!" she shouted. "Quartz, wait!"

There was no reply. Yaz stopped, and waited for Graham to catch up. He bent over for a while, catching his breath, muttering about having a stitch. When he was able, he looked up again, and blinked. "Where's Quartz?"

"Gone," said Yaz, grimly. "Brought us exactly where he wanted us, I imagine."

Behind them, they heard footsteps; low voices calling out: *Have we missed them? Which way did they go?* Yaz, looking back, thought she caught a glimmer of green in the darkness. The Greenwatch.

"Come on," whispered Yaz. "We've got to try and get away."

Graham sucked in a deep breath. "All right, Yaz, love, doing my best!"

"I know." She patted his arm. "Are you going to be OK?"

"I'll be fine."

They hurried through the darkness, listening out for any pursuers.

"This is like that film of Ryan's," Graham said.

"You know a lot about Ryan's films," said Yaz, with a small laugh. "Almost like they're your films too!"

"Well, you try to take an interest, don't you? Keep an eye on what they're watching."

"So what happens next?" said Yaz. "In that film of Ryan's."

"Bloomin' big spider," said Graham.

"Not again!" She shuddered. "Imagine what the spiders must be like round here. They'd have diamond claws or stony shells or something."

"We'd get past it somehow," said Graham.

"At least I was right about something," said Yaz.

"Oh yeah?"

"Quartz wasn't to be trusted."

Graham frowned. "He might just have lost us. It might have been a mistake…"

"Do you want my theory?" said Yaz.

"Go on."

"I think he's playing both sides," said Yaz. "Powerful people do that all over, don't they? Keep in with both sides so that they're always backing the winner. Why should here be any different?"

"We'll see," said Graham, peaceably.

They could hear the footsteps, drawing closer; the voices, getting louder. Yaz looked around wildly. "We could run up and down these tunnels forever," she whispered.

"Come on," said Graham, comfortingly. "You never know what's round the next corner."

Round the next corner, the passage ended at a T-junction. Yaz peered into the darkness, both ways. "Take your pick," she said.

"May as well go right," said Graham. "Better than wrong."

They crept down the right-hand passage. After a little way, it began to curve round ahead of them. "I don't like this," said Yaz. "Never a good idea to be walking without knowing what's in front—"

They saw a flicker of lights on the wall. "Is that from the rocks?" said Graham. "Or something else?"

"I don't know," said Yaz. She gestured to Graham to stand still, and then inched her way forwards. She stopped dead when she heard voices up ahead.

"Not good news, I suppose?" whispered Graham.

Yaz ran back to him. "No. Bad news. Let's go back."

From behind her, Yaz heard someone call out. "That's them!"

"They heard us!" she said to Graham, and, grabbing his arm, pulled him off. "Run!"

They ran as quickly as they could, but their pursuers were soon gaining ground. "Stop! In Emerald's name, stop!"

"No chance!" shouted Graham. "Come on, Yaz, put a spurt on!"

Something came rustling through the air behind them; a shower of small stones. One or two hit Yaz on the arm; they were razor-sharp, and she cried out.

"You all right?" Graham shouted.

"I'm fine, just – watch out!" she yelled. Another shower of stones came at them. "Cover your face, Graham!"

Graham did what she said, but it sent him off balance. He came crashing down on the ground. Yaz pulled up and dashed back to help him. He wasn't even back on his feet by the time their pursuers reached them. Yaz looked up and round. Half-a-dozen rock people, huge and deeply alien, moving into a circle around them. Some were carrying the long crystal weapons; others had handfuls of gravel.

"Sorry, Yaz," said Graham. "Not as quick on my feet as I used to be…"

"It's all right," she said. "They would have got us eventually." She turned to face their captors, her eyes flashing. "All right!" she said. "You've got us!! What are you going to do to us?"

The forest ended, suddenly. The trees and plants came to a stop, and so did the Doctor, Ryan, and Ash. They could simply go no further.

The way ahead was barred by what seemed, at first look, to be a waterfall, blue and white rippling as far as the eye could see, up and down and left and right. But there was something eerily still about the whole display.

"That's funny," said Ryan. "It's not making any noise."

The Doctor was already halfway towards it. "Ah, good, you noticed that."

"Careful!" Ryan called to her. "It could be hot."

"I don't think so," said the Doctor. She reached out and touched the waterfall, and, at her touch, some of it crumbled away and fell to the ground. "This is all stone," she said. "Chippings, or shavings. Ash, did your people make this?"

Ash, coming to join her, shook her head.

Ryan grabbed a handful of chippings and took a closer look. "You know what this reminds me of, Doctor? One of those big slag heaps you get near a mine."

She nodded. "I was thinking that too." She frowned. "Who dumps a whole pile of chippings in the middle of a forest…?"

Suddenly there was an ominous rumbling from above. "Oops," said the Doctor. "We might have."

Ryan felt some small stones land on his head. The Doctor grabbed his hand and they started to run back towards the edge of the forest. Ryan looked round wildly. "Ash," he said. "Where's Ash?"

"Oh no," murmured the Doctor.

Looking back towards the slag heap, Ryan saw that Ash had walked further along, and was rummaging around in some foliage there. "Ash!" he cried. "Get away!"

She started at the sound of his voice, and then saw where he was pointing and looked up. Her sharp eyes widened.

"Get away!" yelled the Doctor, but too late – the face of the stony waterfall began to slip, and a huge pile of stones came cascading down. Ryan watched in horror as Ash fell to her knees under their weight, and was soon covered. After what seemed like an age, the rock fall stopped, and there was another, terrible silence.

"We've got to get her out!" said Ryan.

"Wait a moment," said the Doctor.

"She might be hurt!"

"We'll be no use to her if we find ourselves beneath a secondary fall!"

The Doctor pulled out the sonic, and Ryan tried to be patient while she took some readings. "All right," she said, "I think it's safe now. Come on!"

They both dashed off. They were partway there when the pile of rock under which she was buried began to shift. Two strong arms pushed and punched up, and then the top of Ash's head emerged, and by the time Ryan and the Doctor reached her, she was standing there, unharmed, but blinking. "Wow" said Ryan, "you're tough."

Ash looked over her carapace. "A few scrapes and scratches. Nothing major. Doctor," she said. She pointed to where some foliage was still visible behind the rocks. "I was tugging at this. I'm sure there's a passageway behind it."

The Doctor peered towards where she was pointing, and grinned. "We should take a look," she said.

"But how do we move all this?" Ryan said. "Without bringing another avalanche down on us?"

"Well, we're gonna have to risk it if we want to keep on!" the Doctor said.

Ryan looked up doubtfully. "Maybe there's another path somewhere? Off into the forest again?"

But Ash was already tugging again at the foliage. "Here!" she said. "Look!"

She was right. Just visible through the threads and squishy thick veins of fungi, was a passage, narrow, and very dark.

Overhead, there was another rumbling sound. Ryan, Ash and the Doctor pulled wildly at the foliage, then dived inside the passage. Looking back, Ryan saw a small fall of stones, like a spring shower. "We're not going to get sealed in, are we?" he said, anxiously.

"I can force a way through," said Ash, confidently.

"Not if that whole pile comes down!"

"Don't worry, Ryan," the Doctor said, cheerily. "Look, it's already stopped."

She was right. Ryan heaved a sigh of relief. He could still see a way back.

"Well," said the Doctor. "What are we waiting for!"

She plunged on, holding her sonic up so that it shone a faint light ahead. Ryan followed, and Ash came behind. It was comfortably wide and high enough for even Ryan to walk upright, although he still felt claustrophobic. "Any chance of some more light, Doctor? What's the battery life on that thing?"

"Good enough," she said, and the light became brighter. "Oh," she said. "Look up."

Ryan looked up. They were standing underneath a huge hole and, even with the light from the sonic, he couldn't see how high it went. The Doctor held the sonic up into the hole as far as she could reach, and took some readings. Ryan took the chance to look around.

"That," the Doctor said at last, "goes up very high. Very high indeed…" She touched the walls of the shaft. "And this is smooth, as if a machine had made it… Hmm."

"Doctor," Ryan called over to her, "what's all this?"

She came to look. He pointed with the toe of his boot to some bits and pieces of clutter that were lying on the floor. "These are metal," he said. "Not rock."

"I think they're pieces of broken tech," said the Doctor. "Temperature gauges, that kind of thing. Ash, does any of this look familiar?"

She shook her head. "Nothing I recognise."

"Hmm," said the Doctor. "Could you take another look up that shaft? See what you think?"

Ash nodded and went ahead. Ryan lowered his voice. "All this stuff. Those gadgets there, and that hole over there… Ash's people couldn't have made them, could they? Everything they make is from rock or crystal, or those fibres."

The Doctor smiled. "Well worked out. No, they're not from in here, I think; not from inside the sphere. And…" She ran the sonic over them. "Judging from the metals they use, they're not from up on the surface either. There's not enough of any of this kind of metal on this world to make all this."

"So someone else has been here already," said Ryan. "From up on the surface."

"Beginning to look that way, isn't it? Question is – are they still here? The TARDIS didn't scan the whole planetary surface," she said. "Just enough to make sure it could sustain life – our life."

"So up that shaft we might come face to face with an invading army?"

The Doctor frowned. "Just cos they're aliens doesn't mean they're invading."

"Well, no—"

"*We're* aliens, and *we're* not invading," the Doctor said.

"No, of course we're not!" said Ryan.

"Your films and your telly give you a really funny idea of aliens, you know," said the Doctor. "It's really alienist, your culture. Always seeing a threat when there isn't one." She thought about that. "Isn't *always* one. I mean, there have been quite a lot of alien invasions of Earth, but that doesn't mean every single species is hurrying about space looking to invade the next planet they come to. I mean," she held out her hands, "*I'm* not, am I?"

"No," said Ryan, "but people here are still suspicious of us, aren't they? *They* see us as a threat."

The Doctor sighed. "All I'm saying is – you can't leap from a couple of bits of metal on the floor to full-blown imperialist aggression. Leave that kind of thing to archaeologists."

Ash came back, smiling. "I think I've found something," she said. "Come and see."

They followed her.

"There's something up there," she said. "Some kind of box, I think. I found these strange tendrils, hanging down."

They were metal chains. Ryan tugged at one, gently. High up above, something clanked, rustily.

"Ryan," said the Doctor, "it's not always a good idea to stand underneath a huge shaft and pull the first chain you lay your hands on."

The rusty clanking grew louder.

"Drums in the deep," said Ryan.

"Also, I've been meaning to have a word with you about your policy towards buttons—"

"Doctor!" Ryan yelled. "*Move!*"

He practically jumped into her arms, and both staggered away as a huge metal cage came rattling down and crashed on the ground where he had been standing. When the dust had settled, they all peered inside the cage. On the floor lay another stone tablet.

Ash reached inside the cage and pulled the tablet out. Ryan and the Doctor peered over her shoulders to look. Ryan thought he could only make out a few flecks of mica this time.

"What does it say?" he said.

"Have a guess," said the Doctor.

Ryan looked at the metal cage, which really did look very rusty. "I'm gonna guess it says, 'Come on up'."

"Bingo," said the Doctor. "Shall we give it a go?"

Four Greenwatch marched ahead of Yaz and Graham; four marched behind. Yaz glanced over her shoulder and saw hard, stony faces; implacable and emotionless. Ahead, the backs of their captors were like boulders, impassable. The lights on the rocks around them glanced off them, making them glow like Hallowe'en decorations. She shuddered. There was no way past these people; there was no way she and Graham could possibly fight their way through. It would be like trying to punch your way through a mountain.

"I notice they're not taking us above ground," Graham whispered.

"Don't want to show us to ordinary people," said Yaz. She raised her voice slightly, sounding more confident than she felt. "Don't want to admit the evidence in front of their own eyes."

At length, they came to a huge carved doorway, guarded by two more Greenwatch. Lanterns stood on either side of the door, huge emeralds cut with many faces, sending green light shimmering across the walls.

"Well, this looks like someone's headquarters," Yaz said. "Wonder who it could be, with all this green light?"

The guards moved aside to let their party enter. They came into a passageway hewn out of white stone, but lit, again, so that the walls shone green. They came to another guarded door and, passing through this, came out into a huge white hall.

At the far end, waiting for them, was someone who could only be Emerald.

She was smaller than Yaz had expected, having heard so much about her, almost petite. But she would stand out, even in a room of these remarkable people. Every facet of her seemed to have been cut to perfection; every angle on her considered and finessed for the best effect. On her forehead, like a crown, there was a single red gem. When she moved, she shimmered, and light glanced from her; green light, with the occasional flash of red. Yaz realised her eyes had started watering from the quick shifts in the light. Emerald certainly knew how to disconcert. Yaz summoned up all her wits, and all her training, and all she had learned from her travels with the Doctor so far, tried to speak as plainly and as honestly as possible. She planted both feet firmly on the ground, and crossed her arms behind her back.

"I know that we come as big shock," she said. "We're strangers here – and I know how strange we look! We know how close knit your community is, how frightening we must seem. But we really don't mean you any harm. We're here to help you!"

Emerald leaned forward. The light danced from the garnet on her forehead. "Why do you think we need your help?"

"You must know what's happening," said Graham.

"Must I?"

"The steaming pools of liquid," said Yaz. "The drying seas. The cracks in the sphere of the world."

"What about them?" Emerald said.

"They're not good news, you know," said Graham.

"They're not news at all," said Emerald.

Yaz and Graham gave each other puzzled looks. Graham said, "So, er, what are you doing about them?"

Very softly, Emerald began to laugh.

"What's funny?" said Graham.

"You are," said Emerald. "Both of you. Strangers to this world, by your admission. How long have you been here? It's hardly any time since your blue box arrived. You're not even sure what food and drink you can have."

Oh, thought Yaz. *Quartz really did tell her everything.*

"I'm the ruler here," said Emerald. "I know everything that happens within my sphere of influence. I know everything Basalt said, everything he believed, and everything he tried. And yet, you two believe that you can tell me what I should do."

Yaz shook her head. "You know what's happening here, within the sphere of the world. But I don't think you have any idea what goes on beyond it. You know that the outside world is breaking through, but you don't know what to do about it. And that terrifies you, doesn't it?"

The garnet flashed.

"Yaz," murmured Graham. "I'm not sure this is helping."

"You need to stop pretending that nothing is happening," said Yaz, urgently, while she had a chance. "You need to tell people the truth!"

Emerald turned on her. "And what do you think they would do, if they knew that the world was ending?"

There it is, thought Yaz.

"It's bad enough that there are rumours going around that there are strange people here," Emerald said. "What do you think would happen if people knew the whole truth? There'd be panic, chaos—"

"Perhaps you should have more trust in people," Yaz said. "Yes, there's always someone who panics, but I've seen people in a crisis, and they can be great, they can be brilliant – as long as someone leads them properly!"

There was a silence.

"Oh crumbs," muttered Graham. "I think that's torn it."

"I see," said Emerald. "My leadership is at fault."

"We can help," said Yaz, softening her tone. "Please, if you have it – let us have our blue box back. There'll be something inside that we can use, I'm sure—"

But Emerald was no longer listening. She waved her hands, and the Greenwatch pulled Yaz and Graham away. Yaz called out, "Please! We can help you!"

"Save your energy, Yaz love," said Graham, resignedly. "I think we're about to add another dungeon to our collection."

Ryan eyed the rusty metal cage thoughtfully. "What do you think, Doctor? Is it safe?"

"Oh no," said the Doctor. "No, I shouldn't think so, not in the slightest!"

Ryan sighed. "In that case I guess we *have* to get inside then."

The Doctor grinned. "Me, first!"

Ash and Ryan held the cage steady while the Doctor entered. "All right," she said. "Nothing's broken yet. I think we can try someone else."

Ryan went in next. The cage tilted slightly, but the mesh floor turned out to be surprisingly robust. Ash climbed in next and, once they had the balance right, everything stayed solid.

"Good craftsmanship," said the Doctor, running the sonic over the mesh.

"What do you think this button does?" said Ash, pointing to a panel on the wall.

Ryan reached out and pressed it. With a clank and a groan, the lift shot up, sending the three friends crashing back against the mesh walls of the cage.

"Ryan!" shouted the Doctor. "Never, *ever* press random buttons!"

"You do it all the time!"

"That's different!" said the Doctor.

"How?" said Ryan.

"Because that's me!"

"The floor's holding!" Ash called out. "I think we're all right!"

And it turned out they were. Once the initial shock was over, they realised they were racing upwards at a great pace.

"Oh, this is more like it," said the Doctor. "Hurray for the marvels of mechanisation!"

"Much better than walking," said Ryan.

There was a rustle overhead, and Ryan looked up at the mesh roof of the cage. A ruby rat was peering down at them. Ryan had the distinct impression that it was smiling. If not that, it was certainly showing teeth. "Er, Doctor," he said. "Those rats – did you ever work out what their teeth are made of? Anything that might be able to break a chain?"

The Doctor followed Ryan's gaze, saw the rat and leapt to her feet. "Oh no you don't! Hoick me up, Ryan!"

Ryan hoisted her up onto his shoulders, and the Doctor tried to flick the rat away. "Shoo! Go on!"

This, it seemed, only attracted more rats, and they were, as far as Ryan could tell, pretty narked about having their peace disturbed. Now they were swarming around the bottom of the cage. The Doctor jumped down from Ryan's shoulders and then, together with Ash, started to shove the creatures out of the enclosed space. There were easily a dozen rats now, with more appearing every second.

"Where are they *coming* from?" cried Ryan.

"Nesting in the walls," said Ash. "I told you they were beasts!"

"They were fine one at a time!" cried the Doctor.

"They don't always come one at a time!" said Ash.

The lift was still shooting upwards. Suddenly they were past the patch where the rats had been nesting, and, in short order, they had shoved the rest out of the lift. Ryan was about to take a breath, when the lift swayed, shuddered and slowed.

"All that thrashing about didn't do the lift much good," said the Doctor.

"What if it stops working?" asked Ash, a hint of fear creeping into her voice.

"Well," said the Doctor. "That's an interesting question. Option A. It stops dead and we're left suspended in the middle of this shaft. Long climb upwards if that happens! I hope *someone* packed some rope—"

"Or...?" said Ryan, before that one started up again.

"The other option is that we plunge back down in this cage to where we started. I'm not keen on that option. I'm really not keen on *any* option that ends with squelching. I suppose both options might end in a squelch, if you think them through... it's just that one ends in a squelch sooner than the other one."

"I don't like either of those options," said Ash, in a small voice.

The lift shuddered again, and then ground to a halt.

There was a short pause, during which nobody spoke or moved.

"Hello, option A," said Ryan.

The cage rocked again and tilted alarmingly to one side.

"There is the third option," said the Doctor, trying to keep her footing. "Which is a worrying combination of options A and B. We hang around for a while and then we plunge and *then* we squelch."

"Again," said Ryan, "not keen." He looked at Ash. "No squelch for you, I guess."

"No," said Ash. "I'd shatter."

The lift swung about.

And then, slowly, miraculously, it started to move slowly upwards.

"Is it working again?" said Ryan.

"I don't think so..." said the Doctor. "Look up."

Ryan looked up. There were some faint and flickering lights overhead. *Light at the end of the tunnel.* Slowly, the lift came upwards, and halted. Strong arms were holding it steady. The door to the cage was pulled open. Ash cried out for joy.

"Dad!"

"Ah," said the Doctor, scrambling out of the cage and greeting their saviour. "Basalt, I presume?"

Seven

"I'm starting to think," said Graham, "that travelling with the Doctor involves a lot of doing time."

Yaz didn't answer. She was pacing the small room in which they had been locked. Emerald's accusation that Yaz was involving herself in a situation about which she had little knowledge and no right to intervene had hit hard. *But we can see the damage up above,* Yaz thought. *Someone has got to get Emerald to listen!* Others had tried – Basalt for one – and they had got nowhere. Perhaps an outsider saying it would make the difference... And yet, what gave them the right to turn up and start ordering these people about?

"Yaz," said Graham, "sit down, please. You're going to wear yourself out!"

The worse thing was that it all looked so *easy* when the Doctor did it. People got persuaded to a better course of action, were reminded of their better nature... Yaz wanted to be able to do that too. She wanted to show the Doctor what she was made of, how much she had learned and how far she had come, that all the time she had been travelling with her she had been learning from her... Yaz felt that she had been given a job to do, entrusted with a task by the Doctor. What if she had failed, and failed badly? She didn't like that thought at all.

"You know," said Graham, "This is twice we've been locked up since arriving here."

And then there was Quartz. He had handed them over to Emerald so casually, for whatever small advantage that gained him. Money? Influence? Fat lot of good it would do him if the world ended. Yes, Yaz was angry with Quartz, and she was particularly angry with herself for trusting him, for not listening to what her instincts, and the Doctor's, were telling her about him...

"This won't make a difference to your career, will it, Yaz? Locked up again. That can't look good on a copper's record. I don't want this holding you back."

Yaz swung round and came to stand in front of Graham. "Graham, are you seriously suggesting that being held prisoner on an alien planet by rock-people might one day be a bar to me getting promoted?"

"Well, I don't know, do I? What do I know about coppering?"

"You think that if I had a conversation about this with my sergeant we'd get much past the bit about the rock-people?"

"I suppose not," Graham said, cheerfully. "But at least it's stopped you marching and up and down wearing a hole in the floor."

Yaz realised she'd been played, by an expert. Graham was smiling up at her, and she laughed and sat down next to him, her legs pulled up and her hands resting limply on her knees.

"That's better!" he said.

"So," Yaz said. "What are we going to do?"

"Oh, I don't know," said Graham. "We got out of it all right last time, didn't we?"

"Last time someone came and let us out," Yaz said. "I don't think that's going to happen again."

She jumped up again and went over to the door.

"Oh, now don't start that again!"

"I just want a look out…" She peered through a crack in the rock to try to recce the passageway beyond, but she couldn't see much.

Graham sighed. "We just have to sit it out until something comes along. Maybe those guards, that Greenwatch or whatever they call themselves will turn up again and we can jump them—"

"Graham," said Yaz, "I think there's someone opening the door."

Graham stood up, magnificently. "All right," he said. "Now get yourself behind me." He put up his fists. Yaz stifled a laugh. He looked like one of those old-time boxing champs in a black and white film. The rock in front of the door moved back, and a jet-black face looked in. When they saw Yaz and Graham, they smiled, and little fissures of laughter lines deepened around their eyes. Yaz was sure she recognised this person, but she couldn't place them. Whoever they were, they had a green emerald on their chest. They were Greenwatch.

"What do you want?" Yaz said, trying to keep the fear out of her voice.

The watchman looked nervously back down the corridor. "I'm a friend of Basalt. I'm here to help you – help you get away. But you must be quiet!"

Graham put down his fists. "Who says lightning doesn't strike twice?"

"Hmm," said Yaz. "How about, 'once bitten twice shy'?"

Graham was having none of it. "Don't look a gift horse in the mouth."

Yaz gave up. You couldn't beat Graham at the game of clichés. She followed him, reluctantly, into the passageway, and after their new friend.

Ryan and the Doctor watched with delight as Basalt and Ash folded each other into an embrace. "Aw!" said the Doctor. "Family reunion! That's lovely!"

"Doesn't she look like him?" Ryan said.

"Chip off the old block," the Doctor said, earning a groan from Ryan.

Ash pulled her father over to meet her friends. "This is the Doctor, and this is Ryan. They're here to help us." Her voice was shaking with excitement. "Dad, *look* at them!"

Basalt took them both by their hands. "You aren't the first… *others* that I've seen. But you look very different…"

The Doctor was immediately alert. "Others? Where?"

"I'll show you. But first, tell me – are you from the surface? What's there? Have there *always* been others there, others like you?"

"Slightly more complicated than that," said the Doctor. "Let's say... that yours isn't the only world out there."

Basalt thought about this for a moment, and then Ryan had the privilege of seeing a smile of great joy pass over his face. Basalt looked as if all his wildest, most fondly held dreams had at last come. "I see," he said. "Well, the sphere is full of marvels, and ones that we barely know. Why shouldn't there be even more than I dared hope was possible?"

The Doctor beamed at him. "I knew I was going to like you!"

He grasped her hand. "And you and your friend have brought Ash all the way here to me," he said. "That makes me particularly grateful."

"Ash did most of the work," said the Doctor. "Led the way, solved your messages."

"You helped, Doctor," she said.

"All we did was hold back the lavasharks and the ruby rats," said Ryan.

"Ah, yes," said Basalt, "all most interesting creatures—"

"Dad," said his daughter, in the universal voice of the child whose parent is on the verge of embarrassing her. "I think we've got more to be thinking about right now?"

"You're quite right," he said, and then hugged her again. "Well done, Ash."

"There were moments when I thought I'd never crack your code," she said.

"Sadly necessary," said Basalt. "If Emerald had followed us, she would have destroyed evidence of our journey, and any advice I left on how to follow. Do you know if she's sent anyone?"

Ash shook her head. "Quartz would have told me if she had."

Her father didn't look so sure. "Quartz," he said, "is complicated. He's been a good friend to me over the years. But he's a good friend of Emerald too. We were all friends, once, although time and the wearing of the world has caused some rifts between us."

"Doctor..." said Ryan, anxiously, thinking of his granddad and of Yasmin.

"I know, Ryan," she said, softly. "Basalt — we've left friends behind in Quartz's care. Will he do them any harm?"

"Harm?" Basalt shook his head. "Oh, no, he wouldn't harm them! No, not Quartz. But he might not give them all the help they need. And he might take them to Emerald."

Ryan looked distraught.

Basalt shook his head. "No, no, she won't hurt them! She's not a monster! She's afraid, yes, afraid of new ideas, and afraid of taking risks. But she wouldn't hurt anyone. She wants to protect us... but..." He sighed. "The time when that was possible is long past."

"Why don't you tell us what you've found, Basalt?" said the Doctor.

"To do that, we have to travel onwards," he said. "Or, more precisely — upwards."

"Have you been to the surface?" the Doctor said.

"No, no — not that far. I'm not sure it would be safe for us." He eyed the friends. "How about you two?"

"We'd most likely be fine," the Doctor said. "I think you'd be fine too."

"Good," Basalt said. He led them away from the shaft, and down towards what turned out to be a wide tunnel, carved through the rock. The Doctor ran her hand along the surface.

"Smooth," she said. "Machined."

"Impressive, isn't it?" said Basalt. "Although not as impressive as what comes next." He led them along the tunnel, and Ryan saw that there was track laid on the ground. "What do you make of this?"

Ryan shrugged. "Looks like a railway to me."

Basalt jumped on his words. "A railway? Is that what you call it? Have you seen these things before? How are they made? What are they used for—?"

"Dad…" said Ash, cutting him off.

"Ah, yes, of course…" Basalt gave a sheepish smile. "But you're familiar with these creations?"

"Ryan comes from a place with a lot of this kind of thing about," said the Doctor. "But even he would have to admit that a train tunnel this far under the surface of a planet is pretty impressive."

"There's the Chunnel," Ryan said.

"Not this deep," said the Doctor.

"Oh, OK. Well, yeah, then I'm impressed. And if the trains run on time I'll be even more impressed."

"A 'train'," said Basalt, trying out the word. "Interesting. I called it the runway."

"It's a good name for it," said the Doctor. "I like anything with 'run' in it!"

They walked along a little further, until they came to what was, recognisably, a train, even if Ryan hadn't seen this design before. "Now this is a very clever thing," said Basalt, as they climbed into the carriage. "Moves about under its own power. Very helpful! I'll make some of these, as soon as I get the chance..."

"Where does it go?" said Ryan.

"Where we need to be," said Basalt. He set the machine in motion. It started slowly, and then began to gather pace.

Ash was amazed, and a little frightened. "Is it safe to go this quickly?"

"It hasn't done any damage yet, so far as I'm aware," said Basalt. "Or, I should say, it hasn't done any further damage."

Ryan settled back in his seat comfortably. This expedition had needed more public transport, as far as he was concerned. He watched the tunnel shoot past. "I wonder how this all got built," he said.

The Doctor was waving her sonic about. "I've been wondering that too," she said. "I think I have an idea... Hmm."

Basalt looked around the carriage in wonder. "So this, too, has come from a world far beyond our own..." He shook his head. "Marvellous. Marvellous."

"Where is everyone else?" said Ash. "There were more of you, weren't there?"

"Everyone got here safely," said Basalt. "They're all at the other shaft."

"*Another* shaft?" said the Doctor.

"You'll see when we get there. And you'll see more," he said. "There's the fissure. That's where most of them will be right now."

"The fissure?" said Ryan. "That doesn't sound good."

"It's not," said Basalt. All his playfulness had disappeared. "It's a calamity."

Yaz and Graham followed their guide as he led them down into the tunnels. As she hurried after him, it came to Yaz, suddenly, who their new friend was. The jet-black shell. The white swirls. "Graham," she whispered. "I know who this is. I think we have a problem."

She put her hand on Graham's arm, and they came to a standstill. Their guide looked round, momentarily confused at the delay, and then he smiled. "Ah. You've remembered who I am." He sounded amused. "I believe I have one of those faces. People forget. It comes in handy, sometimes."

"You were at Quartz's," Yaz said, coldly. "You sat at the back and you didn't speak much. Were you the one who gave us away?"

"Oh yeah..." said Graham. "I remember you now!"

Their guide shook his head. "It wasn't me. I'm Onyx, by the way, if you'd like a name."

Yaz looked at the rock creature with deep suspicion. "So if it wasn't you, who was it? And why do you have that?" She pointed to the emerald he was wearing.

"This?" He patted the green stone. "Well, that's because I'm in the Greenwatch, of course. And to answer your other question, I'm not sure. Probably Lazuli, although

I wouldn't be surprised to discover it was Silver. They liked Basalt's ideas chiefly when there was no risk of them actually turning out to be true."

"And you believe Basalt?"

"Of course," said Onyx. "It's not a question of belief, it's a question of evidence. Basalt showed me what he knew, and how he knew it. Only a fool denies proof, even when it goes against custom." He thought about that. "*Especially* when it goes against custom." He gave his small, wry smile. "I really am a friend, you know."

"But you work for Emerald," Yaz said, doggedly.

"I keep an eye on Emerald," he said. "Emerald's problem is that she doesn't understand how far Basalt's ideas have gone. She thinks she's managed to suppress them. But it's not that easy. It's a small sphere. Word gets around. I'm not the only one. And we can see what's happening! The cracks above and all around. The hot pools, and the dried seas. Like I said – you can't deny the evidence of your own eyes!" Onyx sighed. "I think that Emerald doesn't know what to do, and that frightens her. Every stone has its flaw."

Yaz looked again around the tunnels. "You're taking us back to Quartz's house, aren't you? This is a trick! Graham, we have to go!"

"Please," said Onyx, holding up his hands in a placatory manner. "I know exactly what happened. But Quartz can help. He just wants to talk to you—"

"All right, Yaz," Graham said. "I'll go and talk to him. You wait here. If I'm not back in ten minutes – get on your way."

Yaz looked at Graham, and he had that stubborn look in his eye. The one that said he was going to do it, and that nothing would persuade him otherwise. Which meant that she was stuck. Of course she wasn't going to let Graham go off into the lion's den by himself. "OK. We go together, or not at all." She stomped ahead, down the tunnel that led to Quartz's room. "Let's see what he has to say."

Quartz was waiting for them in the room where they had met the other friends of Basalt. He stood to greet them when they entered. "Yasmin, Graham – I owe you both an apology."

"For giving us up to Emerald?" Yaz shot back. "You're right there!"

"I had good reasons. Or so I thought," Quartz said. "For a long time now, I've been trying to protect Basalt. He's my very old and very dear friend. But…" He smiled. "He doesn't care that everything he says has consequences! Emerald thought he might try to get away – she asked me to watch him. And I did, and every so often, I gave her news of him—"

Yaz shook her head. "Your *friend*…"

"—but not enough to put him at risk. And when he confided in me his plans for his expedition, I kept those secret, and I pretended to Emerald that he had told me nothing, and had gone away without my knowledge."

"And she believed you?" said Graham.

"There are reasons she would." Quartz looked down at his feet. "I'm not proud of them."

"You gave other people away to her, didn't you?" said Yaz.

Quartz nodded. "Including you and Graham," he said. "When I knew that you and your friend the Doctor were going to follow Basalt, I thought this was my chance to get away at last. Find Basalt and help him. When we were cut off from the others…" He sighed. "I let Emerald take you two in order to protect the Doctor's mission. If your friends can find Basalt, or find a way to prevent what's happening…"

"It saved you as well, though, didn't it?" said Yaz.

"That's true," said Quartz.

"So why all this contrition now?"

From the corner of the room, Onyx spoke. "A new crack has opened. It's destroyed an entire settlement."

Yaz imagined the devastating effect of the steaming water. "I'm so sorry," she said.

"Emerald is trying to keep the news quiet," Quartz said, "but she won't be able to."

"Word gets out," said Onyx, grimly. "As I say, it's a small sphere, and getting smaller."

"I thought that with time I could persuade Emerald to change her mind… To listen, to start doing what was needed to save us all," said Quartz.

"But you're running out of time," said Graham.

"And at the cost of many lives," Quartz said. He looked heartbroken. "I was wrong. I let this go on for too long. And now I'm worried that we're too late. That we won't survive this. Yasmin, Graham – don't hold everyone who lives in this poor sphere responsible for my mistakes. Please – help us!"

"Well," Graham said, turning to Yaz. "That is what we're here for."

And Yaz sighed, and softened.

*

The journey took several hours, by Ryan's calculation, although he dozed for much of it. Every time he woke, it was to see the Doctor, sitting upright ahead of him, her sonic held out, studying, observing, learning. Ryan wondered, as he slipped back into sleep, if the Doctor ever slept, or whether there were long hours, when everyone around her was resting, which she had to fill. What did she do? Read? Learn a new instrument? Do mad experiments? Practise her snooker? How did you fill the hours, he wondered, when your hours were limitless? Somehow the Doctor managed it with a grin on her face.

Ryan woke to find the train slowing down. There were lights up ahead. For a brief, sleepy moment he thought he was going to hear the announcement: *"The next station will be... Sheffield... where this train will terminate. Alight here for connections to... Manchester Piccadilly, London St Pancras, the Moons of Jupiter, the Centre of the Earth, and... Doncaster..."*

"Wake up, Ryan," said the Doctor, gently.

The train stopped. They climbed out onto a narrow rocky platform, with a few crystal lanterns hanging around that Ryan recognised as the workmanship of Ash and Basalt's people. He peered ahead. The tunnel, and the track, went on into the darkness. In the distance, he could hear a faint, persistent *thrumming* noise. He pointed up the track. "What's up there?"

"The runway goes some way further," Basalt said. "And then it runs out. It looks like there were plans to go further – but it stops. We came this way months ago. You can imagine how marvellous we thought this all was – all this digging, these machines... Incredible!"

"But?" said Ryan.

"But they've come at a price."

"I think I can guess what that is," said the Doctor. She held up her sonic, and took some readings. "We're more or less above the place where those cracks are showing in the roof of the sphere."

Basalt nodded. "I thought so too."

The tunnel opened out to what was plainly intended to have been another platform, or a storage point for equipment. The ground, Ryan noticed, was damp, almost slick with water. "Doctor," he said, pointing down. "Is that seawater?"

She nodded. "I'm afraid so."

Ahead, there was marked activity. Ryan saw a handful of rock-people, some of them resting, some moving around rocks and stones, others carrying them towards the far end of the tunnel. When they caught sight of Basalt, they waved in greeting. One of them, small and with a pearly sheen, stopped work and hurried towards them.

"Ash!" Pearl cried, in delight – and then saw the Doctor and Ryan. "Oh my."

"Hello," said the Doctor, with a little wave. "We're aliens."

"Nice ones though," said Ryan.

"You don't look much like them," Pearl said doubtfully. One or two of the others had come across to join them, greeting Ash with surprise and joy, and then eyeing the Doctor and Ryan. "No, you're nothing like them at all!"

"We come in all shapes and sizes," said the Doctor.

Basalt led them a short way down the platform. The thrumming noise was still going on; Ryan was starting to get a slight headache.

Basalt stopped in front of a large pile of stones. "Here," he said.

"Ah," said the Doctor, and rubbed her fingers against her temple.

"Four of them," Basalt said. "Dead when we arrived, long dead. We raised a cairn over them."

The Doctor nodded sadly. "And nobody else?"

"Nobody else," said Basalt. "They were very different from us – more like you, but even so, not the same... Smaller, bulkier. I think they had more fingers too. And they didn't have..." He patted the top of his head.

"Hair?" said Ryan.

"Ah. That's what it's called," said Basalt. "Is it part of you, or a covering?"

"Part of us," said the Doctor. "Look." She rubbed her arm, making the hairs prickle up. "Same with Ryan's lot too."

"Most interesting..." said Basalt.

The Doctor frowned. "It's odd, isn't it? That the drilling is still going on."

"Ah!" said Ryan. "That's what that noise is!"

"Yes," said the Doctor, "and it's annoying me already, so I don't know how you and your friends have put up with it for so long, Basalt."

"We've no choice, really," said Basalt. "Come and see."

He led them towards the end of the tunnel, the noise got steadily more persistent. They stopped, and Ryan peered ahead. Crystal lanterns shed some light on what was happening. The machined, fashioned parts of the tunnel ended, almost abruptly, but the gaps in the rock did not. Some were as thin as a piece of paper; but others were wide enough for a person to move along. Some of Basalt's people were heading down these, and Ash, with a nod from her father, headed that way, with Pearl.

"All these cracks, they're part of a larger fissure," said Basalt. "If I were to guess, I'd say there's a trench above here. The world… thins here."

The Doctor, her sonic aloft, was nodding. "Yes, yes – the sea is right above here."

"I thought so," said Basalt. "Sea… a type of liquid, yes? The type that comes through the steaming pools?"

"That's it," said the Doctor. "People like Ryan need water like that to live. But for you?" She shook her head. "Horrible stuff."

"My fear, Doctor, is that there is going to be a flood," Basalt said.

"Yes," she said. "The fissure's weakening, isn't it?"

Basalt nodded.

"You realise that using that lift, and that railway might not be helping," the Doctor said.

"We're fairly sparing," Basalt said. "But we have to plug the gaps somehow…"

"Yes," she said. "But it's worse than that. The seawater's pretty warm down here – thermal currents – but as more and more filters past, the fissure gets weaker, and the water gets colder. Extreme cold meeting extreme hot equals bad. Very bad. Sooner or later, it's going to crack open the sphere of the world down there like a spoon hitting an eggshell." She batted the palm of one hand against the fist of another. "And then – water plus lava. Horrible. A steam explosion. It will tear this world apart."

"I was afraid that was what was going to happen," Basalt. "I suppose it's gratifying to have support for my hypothesis, but I can't exactly call it good news."

Suddenly, from up in one of the larger fissures, there was a yell, and Ash came running out, Pearl not far behind her. "Quick!" yelled Pearl, to the others. "We need help up here!" Two or three others, hearing her cry, grabbed up stones and tools and dashed up the tunnel. Ryan saw a thin trickle of water on the ground.

Ash came to join them. Basalt took her hand. "Are you all right?"

"Yes," she said. She was covered in splashes which were making her arms blister. "Dad, that's not going to hold for much longer—"

"I know," he said. He turned to the Doctor. "What shall we do?

"You've done an amazing job so far," the Doctor said. "Unfamiliar tools, unfamiliar materials. Shoring up that fissure. You've saved lives, I bet."

"But it isn't going to be enough," Basalt said. "Is it?"

"No," she said. "We've got to get to the surface."

Basalt shook his head. "We can't risk that. We can't risk weakening the fissure suddenly – it might go. I can't allow it."

"Basalt," said the Doctor, "this is desperate. You've been waiting for help to come – well I'm that help! Emerald isn't going to give in. Whatever's been happening on the surface is causing this, and it's not going to stop unless someone goes out there and makes it stop. You can't do it. But Ryan and I can. That's why we're here!"

"Dad," said Ash. "She knows what she's doing."

"Glad I've given that impression," said the Doctor, with a grin.

"All right," Basalt said. "I think there's a way up to the surface. There's another shaft, with some of those lifting devices—"

"Could one of those take us to the surface?" said the Doctor.

"It might," said Basalt. "I don't know. We haven't risked it."

"We've gotta try, haven't we?" said Ryan.

The Doctor patted his arm. "That's the kind of thinking I like. All right, Basalt – take us to your lifts."

Eight

Basalt led the Doctor, Ryan and Ash back down to where they had left the little train standing on the platform. Beyond the platform, there was another tunnel, which led to lift shafts similar to the one that they had used before to come up to this level. The Doctor stood beneath one of the dark shafts, and lifted the sonic screwdriver.

"Yes," she said, "this'll take us up to the surface."

"Are you sure it's safe, Doctor?" said Ryan.

"I think we have to take the risk," she said. "We'll go slow, and try not to put too much strain on the lift and the shaft. What do you think – ready for a ride? See where we end up?"

Ryan found he was more than ready. Now that the chance of going outside had presented itself, he realised suddenly how much he was missing sunlight, and a limitless sky, and the feeling of fresh air upon his face. This was a marvellous world down here within the sphere; it was vivid and unusual, but it also felt static and unchanging. Claustrophobic. He would be glad to stand outside again – even not knowing what they might find up there.

"I'm ready," he said, and turned to Ash. "Are you coming?"

She shook her head. "I'm needed here," she said, "to help shore up the fissure." She suddenly folded her arms around him. Ryan hugged her back. He'd expected her to feel cold and hard, but instead she was warm and supple. He was going to miss her. She was so strong and so calm. "Take care of yourself, Ash," he said. She nodded, and then turned to the Doctor and hugged her too.

"Come back safely," Ash said.

Basalt and Ash watched as the Doctor and Ryan climbed into the big wire mesh cage. They were soon on their way, heading upwards. The Doctor found a keypad, and played with some of the buttons until they were going at a steady pace. Ryan, looking down, saw Ash, her face flecked with glints of silvery mica, waving up them, until the darkness took her, and he and the Doctor were alone, heading up to uncertainty.

Yaz was keen to go and find the TARDIS but Onyx refused to help. "Emerald is waiting for you to come for it," he said. "It's locked away, and it's guarded. We need to go to Basalt's study."

"Oh," said Graham, "you know about that? I thought it was a big secret."

"It is a secret," said Quartz. "Only a handful of us know where it is."

"And has anyone told that to Emerald?" said Yaz, pointedly.

"Absolutely not," said Onyx. His tone, which was usually playful, was deadly serious. "She would destroy everything in there. She is more desperate than she has ever been."

"So what if we're followed there?" said Graham.

"We won't be," said Onyx.

"It's a long way," said Yaz, doubtfully.

"But there might be something there that can help us," said Quartz.

Reluctantly, then, Yaz and Graham agreed. Onyx proved to be a capable guide. When they reached the tunnel, everything was quiet and, inside, the big chamber was very much how they had left it, all that time ago. Yaz wondered how many days it was – Earth days – since they had set out on their expedition, and been forced to split away from the others. She had lost track of time completely in this strange, lightless world, catching sleep when she could, resting when either she or Graham got tired.

"Is there something in particular you were looking for, Quartz?" Graham said. "Perhaps there's a file somewhere."

Quartz waved his arms hopelessly, taking in the chaos. "If Basalt had a filing system, it was known only to him," he said. "And looking at this mess, I'm not sure *he* knew where everything was either, or why he kept things anyway. Who in their right mind has a ruby rat as a pet?"

"Basalt always seemed to have a thousand projects going on," Onyx said. "Who knows what we might find?"

"You'll know what you want when you see it, eh?" said Graham.

Quartz and Onyx busied themselves at the long stone table, hoping to find what Basalt had been working on most recently. Graham explored some of the display trays, where strange crystals were laid out in no immediately decipherable pattern. Yaz walked through the chamber to the far side, where she found an alcove containing long sets of crystals hanging by threads from the roof. They swayed as she moved close to them.

"Hey," she called out. "What's this?"

Graham came for a closer look. "Look like wind chimes," he said.

"I always found them annoying," said Yaz.

"Grace had some," Graham said, more to himself than anything.

"Oh, I'm sorry, Graham, I didn't mean—"

"Don't worry, I know you didn't!" Graham thought for a minute, and then grinned. "Do you know what – I found them annoying too."

Yaz reached out to touch the nearest hanging crystals. They swayed and struck each other, and they did indeed sound out, melodically. "Much nicer than wind chimes," she said.

"Yes, but what about at three o'clock in the morning?" said Graham. "Never quite got Grace to understand that. She slept like a queen."

Yaz put her arm around him and gave him a hug.

Quartz came to join them. "Ah," he said. "Basalt's library."

"His *library*?" said Yaz.

"The combinations of sounds are meaningful," said Quartz.

Quartz's hands were moving quickly across the chimes, a sweet symphony. Like skim-reading, Yaz thought.

"You do know what you're looking for, don't you?" she said.

He frowned. "You have to know how to strike them in the same way. I wish Basalt hadn't always been so keen on using so many codes!"

"To be fair," said Yaz, "there *was* someone informing on him."

Quartz looked embarrassed, and stopped skimming the chimes. "He *was* working on something new before he left," he said. "But we hadn't tried it out, and I'm not sure whether it works. It was a way to use certain properties of crystals to be able to speak at long distances…"

Yaz and Graham exchanged a look. "A communicator?" said Graham. "Why didn't you mention this before?"

Quartz looked shifty. "For one thing, I didn't know if Basalt had got it to work."

"Oh yes?" said Graham. "And the other thing?"

"Emerald knows about it," said Quartz.

"Because you told her, I suppose?" said Yaz.

"It hasn't been easy here," Quartz said, defensively. "I knew Basalt was leaving. And Emerald knew something was going on. I let her know about the speaking crystals so that she wouldn't get wind of his plans to leave."

"It wasn't a simple matter, you know," said Onyx, "getting a dozen people out of the City and on their way. I'm amazed we got away with it."

"All right, let's not get into judging right now," said Graham, peaceably. "Let's keep ourselves focused on the job. If there *is* a way to get in touch with Basalt, then that's a big help."

Quartz carried searching through the library, and then, he and Onyx picked out a couple of crystals and took them over to the cluttered stone table. He made them play some sounds to him, and nodded. "Basalt's notes on the project," Quartz explained to Yaz and Graham. He and Onyx hurried around the chamber, finding other crystals and bringing them back to set up an elaborate structure. Quartz warmed a few of them within his hands and, slowly, that heat diffused through the other crystals, powering them up. He set up the crystals in a line, facing the stone wall, then placed the largest of the stones in front of him, and began to shift it around in his hands. The crystal began to hum. An image appeared on the wall opposite, hazy at first, but slowly coming into focus. It was a face, dark and stony, with flecks of mica.

"Is that Ash?" said Yaz, and then the image became clear. "No, it's—"

"Basalt," said Quartz.

Basalt's eyes flicked from one side to the other, taking in the room, and who was present. "*Ah, Quartz,*" he said. "*I wondered when you'd get this working.*"

"You didn't make it easy, you know."

"*No, well, it's been a difficult time. Tell me, have you picked sides yet?*"

Quartz opened his mouth to speak, but Basalt hadn't finished yet.

"*Don't worry, old friend,*" he said. "*I know what you were trying to do. I forgive you, and you must forgive me for making good use of all your power and possessions to be able to do the work I wanted to do. I kept you close, and I told you what I wanted Emerald to hear.*"

Quartz's mouth was opening and closing without making any sound. Graham chuckled. "You've been well and truly played, mate!"

Basalt's eyes flicked over to look at him. This was very odd, Yaz thought; like watching an old lantern show.

"*Ah!*" said Basalt. "*Now that is a most unusual face. I imagine that these must be your other friends, Ash.*"

The image on the wall blurred and shook, and then a familiar face appeared where Basalt's had been. "*Hello, Graham. Hello, Yaz,*" said Ash. "*Isn't my father clever?*"

"Extremely clever," said Yaz. She glanced at Quartz, who looked very subdued. "Even cleverer than people thought."

"It's so good to see you," said Graham. "Where's Ryan and the Doctor? Are they OK?"

Ash looked worried. "*They've gone up to the surface.*"

"How did they manage that?" said Yaz.

Quickly, Ash explained about the lifts, and the shafts, and the tunnels – and the bodies. "*We know that someone else has been here. The Doctor and Ryan have gone up to the surface to make contact.*"

Graham sighed. Yaz put her hand on his arm.

Quartz leaned in to speak. "Basalt." He sounded grief-stricken. "I tried my best…"

"*You thought you were acting wisely,*" said Basalt. "*What matters is what you do now.*"

Quartz was not consoled. "It's all gone so far."

"*Much further than you realise,*" said Basalt. "*Listen, all of you. We're in a great deal of danger.*" Speaking quickly, he explained about the deep fissure that his people were only just holding closed.

"So that's what we can see in the roof of the sphere are," said Yaz. "What happens if the fissure cracks wide open?"

"*You've seen the steaming pools, Yaz,*" said Ash. "*More of that – much more, flooding the City and all our islands.*"

"The end of the world," said Graham. "Blimey."

"And the Doctor has gone off to see what she can do," Yaz surmised. "But can *we* do in the meantime?"

"*We need help,*" said Basalt. "*We need materials, people – whatever you can send to help us shore up this fissure and prevent it cracking wide open. Quartz – can you help us? Will you?*"

Yaz turned to Quartz. His grand and smooth confidence had completely gone; he seemed a much humbler, sadder creature than the one she had first met. "Of course," he said, "although we have to avoid Emerald and her people."

Onyx, from one side, said, "I can help with that."

"*There's one more thing,*" said Basalt. "*We need to be careful how much we use these communicators. Quartz, I don't know how much you told Emerald—*"

"Most of it," admitted Quartz.

"*Then she might have worked out a way of knowing when we use them. You should only use them in real need.*" Basalt sighed. "*Though the situation is becoming critical here. We might be past that point already... Be careful!*"

The picture faded.

Ryan felt a gentle *bump*, and then the click of buttons on a keypad. The doors to the lift opened, and they walked out of the cage into the grey light of an alien dawn. Ryan, stepping forwards, found himself looking out across a heathery landscape that whispered with small but busy life. The wind blew through trees and grasses that no human had ever seen, and which did not have – had never had – any name.

Ryan's mind turned to a school trip to Haworth, sandwiches on the bus… He'd almost forgotten, in the fun and mucking about of the day, and the crush and boredom of the big forbidding house, that there had been a brief moment looking out across the empty moors, when his heart was quietly but suddenly moved by the wild beauty of it all. He wondered now whether all his mates had felt the same, but would have died rather than admit it. Daft what you do, he thought. When you were a little kid, you didn't mind getting excited and enthusiastic and gobsmacked when things amazed you, and telling everyone around you how brilliant things were. And then you got older and you tried to forget about all that; you pretended that you were bored or nothing was impressive. And then one day you found yourself, nearly every day, seeing something that blew your mind. He hoped he would never forget this feeling. Perhaps a large part of being really grown-up was remembering to be amazed.

"All quiet, and untouched," he said. "Nobody's spoiled it."

The Doctor stood beside him, looking out across the untamed land.

"Lonely, though," he said. "Big and empty… And yet right beneath our feet there's a whole secret world happening. All that worrying and fighting and keeping secrets. All those amazing creatures and sights—"

"And mushrooms."

"Right, yeah. But out here, there's just the wind and the sunrise, and…"

The Doctor grinned. "There's a poet in you."

Ryan laughed. "Don't be daft!"

Behind them, situated beyond where the lift had come out, a series of low buildings had been constructed. Ryan counted half-a-dozen. Around these were various kinds of machinery, similar in design and feel to the lifts and the train, and the bits and pieces of gadgetry they had seen cluttered below around the foot of the first life. All from the same manufacturer, whoever or whatever that was.

"Hmm," said the Doctor. "Quiet, isn't it?"

"Looks abandoned," Ryan said. "And there was I, all ready for a first contact or a close encounter…"

The Doctor had the sonic out. "No life signs. Energy sources, yeah, and power supplies, but not people…" She frowned. "Let's have a closer look."

They walked towards the nearest building. Close up, it looked half-built: there was no door, and when they peered inside, it was empty. Grasses had grown through the space where the window should have been, and were trailing down the inside walls. The next two or three buildings were in the same state: half-constructed, half-overgrown. When they reached the next building, the biggest, the Doctor's interest was piqued. "Ah, now, this is more like it. A locked door. Signs of life at last."

Ryan watched as she worked at it. "Doctor, this *was* a mine, wasn't it?"

"Yes, but whoever came here abandoned it. Maybe because of whatever accident killed those poor miners."

"So why is the drilling still going on?"

"Dunno. Let's get inside here and see if we can find out."

The door popped open. The Doctor grinned. And then her expression turned to alarm at the sight of a huge golden swarm bursting through the door, buzzing and fizzing.

"Get down!" the Doctor yelled to Ryan. "Cover your face!"

He did what he was told, peeping through between his fingers to see what the Doctor was doing. She was standing with the sonic held up, apparently unafraid of whatever these things were and what they could do to her. After a moment or two, Ryan saw the golden haze around the creatures flicker, like Christmas tree lights on the blink, and then go out. There was a moment's silence, and then a clattering sound as the things fell to the ground. Ryan covered his head completely; the thought of being buried under a pile of dead wasp-like creatures did not appeal. "Doctor!" he shouted. "What's going on?"

"It's all OK," said the Doctor. "You can get up. I've switched them off."

"Switched them *off*?" Ryan jumped up, shaking off the creatures that had fallen on him. "Aren't they, like, bugs or something?" He peered at the pile of them; a heap of little grey...

"Nanobots," said the Doctor. She looked round. "Huh. That's impressive."

"Impressive?"

"They're tiny robots," She knelt down by the pile, waving the sonic around. "Pretty advanced, too. These little things are responsible for building most of what you've seen here.

The shafts, the lifts, the buildings, maybe even the railway and the tunnels."

"How does that work?" said Ryan.

"Well, dragging loads of equipment across space is a real hassle. Takes loads of fuel and it's really boring. So you send along nanobots – tiny robots, you can't see them – that are programmed to use the materials they find here to make the buildings and so on." She struggled for an example. "Like flat-pack furniture. You assemble on arrival."

"A flat-pack mine," said Ryan. "Cool."

"Yup. The nanobots do it all. By the time the people arrive, the place is all set up."

"Why send people at all, when nanobots can do all this?" said Ryan. "And there aren't people here now, are there?"

"No," said the Doctor. "And yet the mine is still running." She peered through the open door, and then grinned back at Ryan. "Shall we find out why?"

They crept inside. It was dark, and windowless, and the Doctor had to hold the sonic out in front of them like a torch.

"Spooky," said Ryan.

They wandered along a corridor, checking out rooms as they went past. "This looks like a command centre," said the Doctor. "Places to sleep, rec rooms, workplaces… Oh, now, this looks useful!"

They had entered a big room with workstations, some with tech and gadgets, recognisably tools or screens where people could do their jobs. Ryan looked around in amazement, while the Doctor started fiddling at a control panel.

"I see it's all right for *you* to press buttons," Ryan said.

"Yeah, but I'm great at pressing buttons," she said. "When it comes to pressing buttons, I'm the best." She thumped a few more, and a little holographic display popped up. Ryan saw strange symbols and diagrams scrolls past. "Here we are," said the Doctor. "Business plan. Yep, this was a mine. The first set of miners arrived. They were here a few weeks and…."

"What happened?" said Ryan.

"They hit an unexpected gas pocket in the mantle," said the Doctor. "Dozens were killed."

"Killed?" Ryan frowned. "But we've been breathing the same air they were…?"

"And we're still here. It's dispersed over time. Or maybe to us it's not fatal at all." The Doctor shrugged. "In any case, it seems that nobody was willing to go back down, not even to get the bodies."

"So they left?" Ryan looked round. "After all this construction and investment?"

"Maybe they decided it wasn't worth carrying on. Maybe the company went bust."

"Maybe a politician decided to close all the mines," said Ryan.

"Whatever the reason, the project stopped – but the drilling didn't. And now the whole planet's on the brink of destruction." The Doctor frowned. "I'd like a word with these people. You can't go around littering planets, dumping your machines on them and leaving them to do all sorts of damage."

"So what do we do?"

"First thing, we turn everything off."

"Won't that attract attention?" said Ryan. "If we start messing around with things, someone might come to find out what's going on."

The Doctor started working at the controls. "Then they can come here and they can talk to me. I have plenty to say to them. Besides, we're running out of time. Basalt and his people can't keep that fissure sealed for much longer—"

"Doctor!" hissed Ryan. "Quiet! Listen!"

They both stopped to listen.

There were footsteps, in the corridor, heading towards them.

Nine

After the connection with Basalt faded, Onyx turned to the others. "We need to get Basalt's work away from here."

Graham looked around at the chaos. "What, *all* of it?"

"As much as we can," said Onyx. "You heard what Basalt said. Emerald might be able to follow those messages to the source. If she comes here…"

Yaz surveyed the room, full of treasures.

"I don't believe she'd destroy all this," said Quartz.

"Believe it, Quartz," said Onyx. "Now, are you going to help me?"

They got to work. Quartz worked quickly through the library, determining with Onyx which projects were most useful, and what crystals or other paraphernalia needed to be saved. Yaz, hunting around, found two large bags, made from the strong fibre that she had seen elsewhere, and she and Graham packed these up with the materials Onyx passed to them. When the bags were full, Onyx tested their weight. They were heavy, but he seemed to think he could manage carrying them.

Graham looked around the study, which was still heaving with Basalt's collections. "We've barely scraped the surface," he said, with a sigh.

"Have a look round for a cellar," said Onyx. "There might be somewhere we can hide more. Meanwhile… I should take all this away. To somewhere safe," he said, with a smile. He turned to Quartz. "I'll be back as soon as I can."

Quartz nodded. "I'll work out what we need to take to Basalt, and where we can find it without attracting Emerald's attention."

"I'll find some people willing to help," Onyx said. He headed towards the door. Yaz followed him, and Onyx turned to her. "Next time you see me, Yaz, I might seem unfriendly."

She frowned. "Unfriendly?"

"But please trust me."

He went off through the door, back into the tunnel that led to the surface. Graham, still rootling around the study, called Yaz over. "Hey, I think there's something under here!"

Graham had found a large stone on the floor that was loose, and seemed to be covering something. When they moved it, they found steps down into a tiny cellar, barely tall enough for them both to stand up in. But it was space, and it was hidden.

"Excellent poking around, Graham!" said Yaz. Under Quartz's instructions, they bundled up more of Basalt's work and stashed it in the hideaway. It was tiring work, and after a while, Graham stopped.

"I'm wiped out," he said. "We should rest. We've got a journey ahead of us, if we're going to find Basalt."

Yaz nodded. Graham found some hammocks, made from the tough fibre that the rock-people liked to use, and he slung these up, and they both lay down. Yaz couldn't rest. She was aware of Quartz, on the other side of the room, still busy working out materials they needed, and routes to smuggle them out of the City and up to Basalt. Yaz sighed. She liked to be in the thick of action, making decisions, making things happen, making things change. Waiting for others was not in Yaz's nature.

Graham was already asleep. Yaz looked over at him, eyes shut, breathing deeply, and wished she could switch off for a little while too.

Instead, she got up and wandered round the study. The room felt barer now, although there was still a great deal that they hadn't been able to hide. She looked up. There was a skylight in the roof above, and she looked up into the dark of the night cycle. The white streaks – the cracks – looked even bigger. She sighed, and resumed pacing. When she passed Graham's way again, he opened one eye and said, "I'm never going to get any sleep with you marching about."

"Sorry."

Graham sighed. "Ah well," he said. "No sleep for the wicked." He stood up, and followed her over to the skylight, then frowned. "Is it me, or are there more of those cracks?"

"Lots more," said Yaz. "Graham, we need the TARDIS. If we can only get inside, it would make a perfect shelter."

"The whole population would be safe and sound in there… if we can open the doors." He nodded decisively. "Got to be worth a try."

They went over to Quartz. He looked up in surprise; he'd been deep in his plans for some time.

"We want to get back to the TARDIS," said Yaz.

"The blue box," Graham explained. "If those cracks in the sky get any bigger, your people are gonna need a proper roof over their heads."

Quartz shook his head, troubled. "I don't know what to suggest. Onyx knows where the blue box is, but I don't. We should wait for him to come back—"

"You can wait," Yaz said shortly, "but we're—"

From the far side of the room, a humming sound began.

"What's that?" whispered Graham.

Quartz gathered himself first. "The crystals. Someone is trying to speak to us." He headed over to where the crystals still stood in a line. "Perhaps it's Basalt?"

"Or Emerald!" said Yaz.

Quartz's hand hesitated for a moment. Then he picked up the crystal.

In the control centre on the planet's surface, Ryan looked around wildly. "Doctor," he whispered, "there's someone coming!"

There was nowhere to hide – the Doctor looked steely, and held the sonic out in front of her.

The footsteps stopped. Everything went very quiet. The Doctor put the sonic away.

"All right," she called out, "we know you're there. Whoever you are – we're not here to harm anyone. All we want to do is talk."

A figure came through the door.

Ryan breathed a sigh of relief. "Ash! How did you get here?"

She stared at him with wide, glassy eyes, like someone in shock. "There's… there's more than one lift, remember?"

"I'm guessing your first steps on the surface are something you'll never forget." The Doctor grinned. "How'd you like it?"

"The openness, the space, the taste of the air, the far nothingness of the sky. It's—"

"Amazing, yeah?" said Ryan.

"Frightening." She gave a small smile. "But illuminating." Though Ash didn't say as much, Ryan guessed she was glad for the roof over her head as she surveyed the gently humming workstations. "What are *they*? What *is* this place?"

"It's a control centre for a mining operation," said the Doctor.

Ash blinked. "None of that made sense," she said. "What's mining?"

"You know," Ryan said, "digging precious stones and metals up from the ground…" He thought about Ash's world, and the sheer abundance of stones and metals lying to hand. "Don't you dig, then?"

"No," she said. "We harvest."

"Other places, other worlds, they don't have the same resources as you do here. They don't have all these gems and stones and everything."

"Exactly the opposite in some places," said the Doctor. "Or maybe they've used up what they had. That could make a world like yours very attractive."

"So they'd *take* what we have?" Ash's eyes widened in shock.

"Nobody is taking anything from anyone as long as I'm here," said the Doctor quietly, "believe me."

Ryan shivered a little. The Doctor was almost entirely fun, almost all of the time – and then she'd do or say something, and you remembered that while this was a mate, she was also an alien with amazing powers that he knew hardly anything about. He'd seen the Doctor at work. He absolutely believed that she could topple empires as if they were a tower built of dominoes.

"Ash, what's that crystal you're holding?" the Doctor asked brightly.

She started. "Oh! This is my whole reason for coming here. Something my father was working on. It means we can speak at distance to each other."

She held out the crystal, and the Doctor took it. "A communicator! I've said it before, but he really *is* clever, your dad! What's the range on this?"

"We spoke to Quartz," Ash said. "And Graham and Yaz."

"Are they OK?" said Ryan.

"They're fine! My father and I thought you should speak to them, Doctor. But it can't be for long. Emerald knows about these crystals. She might know how to trace the transmissions."

Ash activated the crystal. And there, miraculously, on the wall opposite, Ryan saw his granddad's face.

Graham's expression turned from worry into joy. *"Ryan! Good to see ya! And you, Doc – don't want to leave you out!"*

Quickly, they brought Yaz and Graham up to speed about what had been happening. Yaz was jealous. *"Lavasharks! Dangerous mines! Spooky forests! All we've had is running along tunnels and another dungeon. Your standard stuff."*

"On the downside," said Ryan. "I'll never be able to look at a mushroom in the same way again."

"So what's the surface like?" said Graham.

"Looks like Yorkshire," said Ryan.

"Typical," said Graham. *"You come all this way, and you may as well have stayed at home."*

"Anyway – you know the mine, and all these buildings, right?" said Ryan. "Built by robots."

"Nanobots," said the Doctor.

"Tiny robots," said Ryan.

"The mining has been causing all the cracks," said Yaz, urgently. *"Doctor, they're getting so much worse. I want to find the TARDIS."*

"I don't want you putting yourselves in danger," the Doctor said.

"We're in danger anyway!" said Yaz.

The Doctor sighed. "All right," she said. "Meanwhile, we'll see if anyone turns up—"

She stopped speaking. In the background, where Yaz and Graham were, there was a lot of noise, as if more people had entered the room. Ryan heard Quartz, from off, say, *"How dare you come in here without permission!"*

Yaz hissed, *"Doctor, it's the Greenwatch!"*

The picture on the wall flickered, and was gone.

"Yaz!" Ryan turned to the Doctor. "Tell me the communicator is broken?" She shook her head, and Ryan thumped his hand against the console. He wanted to be there, to help, but it was impossible. He was the depth of a planet away.

"I'll tell you what, Ryan," said the Doctor. There was a steely look in her eye. "I think I'm ready to talk to Emerald now."

Yaz and Graham looked around desperately for somewhere to hide, as Quartz held the Greenwatch at bay at the door to the tunnel. "What about the cellar?" Graham whispered. "Where we've hidden Basalt's library?"

Yaz shook her head. "Not big enough," she said. "Besides – if they find us, I don't want them finding more of Basalt's work at the same time."

Quartz was shouting now. "Don't you know who I am?" he said. "This is my private property! There'll be consequences for this—"

"Things are changing, Quartz," replied one of the people at the door. He didn't sound particularly upset, Yaz thought. Maybe he was glad to be able to speak his mind to Quartz at last. "This is an emergency. Emerald believes that whatever Basalt was doing here has been causing the cracks in the roof of the world—"

"Oh," whispered Graham. "That's a new one."

"The work done here is what will save us!" Quartz shot back.

Graham pulled Yaz back towards the alcove where Basalt's library had been hanging. "This will hardly hide us for long—"

"No," he said. "But look at this."

Yaz looked over at the wall. "A door!"

"This whole planet seems to be made of secret tunnels," said Graham, yanking the door open. Behind was a narrow passageway, running upwards. Yaz was about to step inside, when a sudden thought sent her dashing back into the study. She ran to the table and lifted the dome from over the ruby rat. It gave her the evil eye, and then jumped off the table. "Go on, little guy, run for the hills," she murmured, as it fled.

"What did you do that for?" Graham whispered, as Yaz hurried back to join him.

She shrugged. "I felt bad for it," she said. "And the Doctor wanted it to go free. So."

She went into the passageway, and Graham came in behind her, pulling the stone door back into place. They hurried along. The passage soon came back up to the surface. "Let's hope there's nobody up there," whispered Yaz, as they clambered up onto open ground.

For the moment, it seemed they were safe. They started to jog across the plain, and then there was a cry, and they knew that the Greenwatch had worked out what was happening.

The chase was on.

Yaz looked ahead. In the distance, heading their way, she saw a dark figure carrying a glimmering crystal rod and wearing a green stone. The figure started to lope towards them, to cut them off.

"Oh dear," said Graham. "We're in trouble…"

Yaz wasn't so sure. The figure drew closer, and she saw that it was Onyx. "Oh!" she cried. "Glad to see you! We're on the run!"

They stopped in front of him, trying to catch their breath. "I'm done with all this running around," gasped Graham. "Isn't there a bus service?"

Yaz turned to speak to Onyx, but he was looking behind her, as his colleagues from the Greenwatch drew closer. He spoke softly and urgently. "You need to trust me now."

Yaz understood. "Is everything safe?"

He gave a small, barely perceptible nod. Then the Greenwatch arrived, and Quartz, not far behind. The other Greenwatch each pressed the flats of their knobbly hands against their green stones, which Yaz took to be a kind of salute. Onyx nodded back. *Oh,* she thought. *He's their boss.* She glanced at him again, and, looking at his stern face, her nerve wavered. Was he really as friendly as he made out?

"Onyx," hissed Quartz.

"Not a pleasant feeling to find yourself betrayed, is it, Quartz?" said Onyx. He turned to the others, and issued some quiet orders, which Yaz couldn't quite catch. Two of them loped off, back in the direction of Basalt's study, leaving two more, and Onyx, behind. If this was a performance, Yaz thought, it was very convincing. Onyx had not yet met her eye again. "Quartz," he said, "you're free to go."

Quartz was dumbstruck. "What?"

"It's just the strangers that Emerald wants," Onyx said. "She's grateful for your service so far, and as a mark of this, she's prepared to let you go free."

"Look at Quartz's face," muttered Graham to Yaz. He chuckled. "Emerald has a bloomin' cheek!"

Quartz was quivering with anger. "How *dare* you!"

"But you're welcome to come along, if you'd prefer," Onyx said.

"Yes, I'll be coming," said Quartz. He turned to Yaz and Graham. "I'm sorry," he said. "Sorry for the mistakes I've made. But I won't leave you in the hands of this traitor." He turned back to Onyx. "I want to speak to Emerald—"

Coolly, Onyx said, "If she has time, I'm sure she'll be willing to have a word or two." He stopped, and looked back across to Basalt's study. And then he nodded, as if satisfied.

Yaz's heart twisted in her chest. "What have you done?" she said to Onyx. "Those Greenwatch – what are they doing in there?"

Onyx didn't reply.

"I imagine," said Quartz, bitterly, "that they're doing Emerald's dirty work for her."

"There won't be much left when they've finished," Onyx agreed, in a calm voice.

Yaz thought of that wonderful space, where Basalt had worked so hard, and made such wonderful discoveries and inventions, being reduced to a pile of broken stones and smashed crystals. They had hidden such a small part of it… She put her hand to her mouth. What had happened to everything Onyx had taken with him? Had that all gone the same way?

"Oh no," breathed Graham. He turned on Onyx. "I don't know if you think this is clever, mate, but it's not. It's out of order. Downright wrong!"

"Emerald said it was dangerous," said Onyx, "and we can't allow dangers, can we?" He sounded rather bored. "Come on," he said. "There's nothing to see here now."

Yaz felt utterly defeated, as if everything she had tried to do had been a failure. She had not learnt her lesson from Quartz, and instead had trusted Onyx, and it had been another mistake. And now she and Graham were captured, and Basalt's work had been destroyed, and their plans to send him help had been found out.

"Don't beat yourself up, Yaz," Graham whispered. "We did our best."

"Not good enough, though, was it?"

"And think about this – we're closer now to the TARDIS than ever. You never know what chance we might get."

Yaz appreciated his optimism, but she couldn't share it. She tried to steel herself for the encounter with Emerald that lay ahead, but when they were brought into her hall, Yaz's heart sank again. They really had nothing to bargain with. As the woman walked towards them, Yaz was struck again at how small she was – smaller than any of her people, and yet they were clearly in thrall to her.

Not Quartz. His eyes were flashing. "How *could* you?" he said. "All of Basalt's work. Everything he did, and learned…" He shook his head. "It's a terrible thing you've done!"

Emerald came to stand in front of him. "Nothing went wrong here until Basalt began conducting his experiments. If we stop that, perhaps we can stop what's happening to the roof of the world."

The Doctor's voice popped into Yaz's head, whispering something, so she said it out loud. "Correlation isn't causation."

Emerald turned her head slightly to look at her. "What did you say?"

"Correlation isn't causation," Yaz said, more confidently. "Just because two things happen roughly at the same time doesn't mean one is causing the other."

"She's right," said Quartz. "And you know she is, Emerald. Basalt didn't cause any of this! He's been trying to warn us – for ages now – and all we did was harass him, and, finally, drive him away."

"And who knows what he's done since then," Emerald shot back. "Everything became worse after he left!"

"He's not the *cause*!" Quartz said. "All this – the cracks, the steaming pools, the drying seas… We know what the cause is now! There's been digging, up on the surface—"

"There's no such thing as the surface," Emerald said firmly.

"Emerald!" Quartz cried out. He turned to point to Yaz and Graham. "Look at them! They're not from this world!"

There were a few mutters from the Greenwatch gathered round, Yaz noticed. "Oops," murmured Graham. "The troops are getting restless."

"We *know* what's causing all our problems!" Quartz went on. "Basalt, Ash, these people – they're trying to help! Trying to save us! Emerald, old friend, dear friend – look at them! Why are you denying the evidence of your own eyes?"

Emerald stood in silence for a while. Was this it? Yaz wondered. Was this the moment when she would admit that she had been wrong, and let them help her at last?

"No," she said at last. "We've destroyed Basalt's work. Now I'm sure we'll see an improvement."

"Some people…" Graham muttered. "How do they always end up in charge?"

"All of these lies have to stop, Quartz," Emerald said. "Basalt's work is destroyed."

Onyx stepped forwards. "Not all of it, Emerald." He turned to Yaz and Graham and gave a small bow. "Basalt's notes and many of his materials have been preserved."

Yaz breathed a sigh of relief. She'd been so afraid that Onyx wouldn't step up to challenge his queen. Graham gave Onyx a discreet thumbs up.

Emerald swung round to face Onyx. "Preserved? But I ordered—"

"What you ordered was vandalism, Emerald," said Quartz, "it was pointless desecration. Nobody doubts that you have the interests of our people at heart – all that you've done to shore up the City against the steaming pools, the help you've given to those left devastated by these changes, the way you have kept people calm. These have all been the actions of a good leader. But now you're risking everything—"

"You're all fools," said Emerald, wearily. "Everything's getting worse, and you've allowed Basalt his way. He's going to kill us all!"

Yaz felt her heart sinking. Were they all going to die because one person wouldn't admit her mistake? How could Emerald's mind be changed?

And then, suddenly, someone else was in the room. Bang in the centre of the room, appearing out of nowhere.

"What is this?" cried Emerald, jumping back as her guards did the same. "How did you get here?"

Graham cheered. "Here she is!"

"Doctor!" said Yaz, in delight. The Doctor turned and waved. She seemed to shimmer slightly, Yaz noticed, and she looked *huge* – at least a foot taller than in real life.

Graham shook his head. "Technology, eh? I've only just worked out the CD player in the car!"

"All right, Yaz!" the Doctor said. "Hiya, Graham! Ryan's here, sends his love…" Her head turned, as if she was speaking to someone who they couldn't see. "What? Well, you *do* send your love…"

"How's she doing this?" Graham said, boggling.

"Some sort of hologram? Who knows?" Yaz grinned. "Here or not, she definitely knows how to make an entrance!"

"Now then – Emerald, isn't it?" The Doctor's image had turned, eyes fixed on the ruler. "It's time we had a talk, don't you think?"

Ten

Emerald's face was a study in fury. "Who are you?" she said. "How *dare* you?"

"I'm the Doctor," said the Doctor. "And how do I dare? Because you've given up, Emerald. You've stopped listening, and you've started lying, and you think you're doing the right thing, but you're wrong."

Emerald gestured to the Greenwatch, standing around. "Take her," she said. "Put her somewhere deep and dark."

"Oh," Graham said. "This should be good!"

Two of Greenwatch moved towards the Doctor, and each tried to take an arm. There was, of course, nothing to hold. They stumbled, and fell, right through the hologram, landing on top of each other.

"What's happening?" said Emerald. "Is this a trick?"

"Oh, it's no trick!" said the Doctor, with a laugh. "Here I am, right in the middle of your City, and you can't touch me. You can't do anything about me. You can't stop me or send me away, and you definitely can't shut me up."

"That's certainly true!" said Graham, cheerfully.

"It's the same with the people who've caused so much harm to your world." The Doctor thrust her hands into the pockets of her long coat. "There's nobody here to fight now, there's nobody here to lock up. The damage has gone on remotely, long after they left. But perhaps the greatest damage now is what you're doing yourself."

Quartz went to stand near Emerald. "Listen to the Doctor," he begged her.

"Hullo, Quartz!" The Doctor waved at him. "Have you picked sides now?"

Quartz nodded stiffly. "I know I made mistakes. I'm trying to rectify them."

"That's what I like to hear! Now, Emerald – it's your turn to do the same. I'm not telling you anything you don't know already: your world – your sphere – has a surface. And that surface has been visited by people from other worlds. They wanted the precious stones and the metals, so they started to dig. But it's gone wrong, and it's cracking the roof of your sphere. Basalt worked most of this out, you know – everything he said was true – and with his help I've been able to work out the rest." She beamed suddenly. "I've got a plan too, if you're ready to hear it. A plan to save everyone here."

Emerald drew closer to the Doctor's hologram. "Stop this!" she cried. "Stop all of this!"

The Doctor shook her head. "I was hoping you'd see sense," she said. "Why is it never straightforward?"

"Some people," said Graham, "just won't listen."

"You're right there, Graham," the Doctor said. "All right, Emerald, reasoning hasn't worked – so let's try another way to get your attention. I know you're planning to cover all this up, and tell people that it's all Basalt's fault. I'm afraid you're too late."

Emerald looked at her in horror. "What do you mean?"

"This picture of me – it's called an avatar, by the way, a holographic avatar – it's not just appearing here, in your stony den. It's appearing right now in every walkway and chamber of your City. They really are clever, the miners who built it. I just had to boost the range and – *whoomph*. Here I am, talking to everyone." The Doctor frowned. "I don't like leaders that tell people deliberate lies. It's best all round if we all start with full information and make some decisions from there." She stopped, and then she grinned and started to wave. "Hello, rock people! I'm the Doctor! I'm an alien from another planet! Just thought I'd get that one out there right away. I'm talking to you from the surface of your own world – up, up, beyond the roof of the sphere. I'm there right now, looking up at the sky. Hey, hang on a minute, a few tweaks with the sonic and you'll see! Oh, you're gonna love this, rock folk!"

There was a crackling and a rustling, and her holographic image went out of focus.

"What's she up to now?" muttered Graham.

And then Yaz understood. Where the Doctor had been standing there was now a landscape opening out in front of them, a quiet world, but remarkable nevertheless to people who had never seen such a thing before. The Doctor was showing the rock-people the surface of the wider world around them.

"Look," said the Doctor. "That's grass, and that's the wind blowing through it, and, hey, look at this!" The image tilted again. "That's the sky! Up, up, and up, a vast space right above you, and if you travel far enough you reach other worlds..."

All around the room, people were murmuring.

"And some of those worlds have people on them – like me!" The landscape disappeared, and the Doctor's avatar popped back up. "It's like Basalt has been saying all these years," the Doctor said. "And now you've seen it with your own eyes. Amazing, isn't it? Anyway, here I am, and I know you're scared right now, what with the pools streaming and the seas drying up and the sky falling in your head – but I'm here to help!"

With a cry, Emerald dashed towards a window. Yaz and Graham followed behind. Looking out, Yaz saw that people were gathering out in the walkways, conferring, some in confusion, more in anger. And there – yes, there! and there, and there! – was the Doctor, or, rather, many Doctors, dotted all over the City, saying exactly what she liked, telling the truth.

"So this is what I'm going to do," said the Doctor. "I've turned off the mining systems, and with luck that'll stop the cracks opening wider for a while. I don't think we've passed the critical point, not yet. But what you all need to do – you strange, marvellous, beautiful people – is to start helping Basalt. Those cracks in the roof of the world above you are widening, opening up into a big fissure. Basalt's been working to keep the fissure closed – to save all your lives – but he and his people can't do it alone any longer. They need material, and they need help." She looked at Quartz. "You'll help, won't you, Quartz?"

"Doctor," he said, "it would be an honour."

"There! Quartz is willing and ready! Talk to Quartz, everyone! He'll get you organised." She turned back to Emerald. "Sorry to bypass you like this. I should probably worry more about due process when overthrowing governments, but we're running short of time, and if we carry on like this, there won't be anywhere or anyone left to govern."

Her image flickered slightly.

"Yaz, Graham – help Quartz. Once we've stopped the drilling and the tunnelling, the lifts and the train should be safer to use. Send Basalt help, as quick as you can!"

"We're on it, Doctor," called Yaz.

"You can count on us!" said Graham.

Her image flickered again, and then was gone.

The Doctor switched off the holographic transmitter and grinned at Ryan and Ash. "I enjoyed that!"

"I could see!" said Ryan. "What do you think's happening back there? Emerald looked pretty furious—"

The Doctor gave a slow smile. "I don't think Emerald will try anything," she said. "I think we've rendered her slightly irrelevant. I'm not sure even the Greenwatch will take orders from her now. If only they'd start answering back…" She clapped her hands together. "Right," she said, heading towards the console. "Let's check the systems are powering down correctly…"

"I feel sorry for Emerald," said Ash, unexpectedly.

"What?" Ryan was amazed. "She tried to destroy your dad's work! She wouldn't listen to him and then she tried to put the blame on him!"

"I know," said Ash. "But she wasn't always like this. She and my father were very good friends, in their youth. They studied together. She was a good leader, once. She was responsible, and thoughtful, and took good care of people. Maybe if the times had been different, if all of this hadn't happened…"

The Doctor, studying the meters on the console, looked up. "It's easy to rule well when times are good," she said. "It's when things get difficult that people show what they're made of."

"I know," said Ash. "It's just… I think my father's ideas frightened her, and of course, they didn't seem *real*, did they? She could see all these problems, and she knew that he could help if he turned his mind to it, come up with ideas to do something practical, and all he did was talk, well, *nonsense*, in her eyes. I think that's why she became so angry. There were serious problems, and as far as she could make out, he wasn't helping."

The Doctor smiled at her. "You've got a generous spirit, Ash."

Ash shrugged. "I just want to be fair."

Ryan nodded at the control panel. "Sorted, Doctor?"

"Only slowing down. The drilling can't be stopped dead, too many safety precautions built in to protect the equipment. I'll see if I can bypass them." She started sonicking at the console. "We need to help your dad shore up that fissure."

"Dragging everything up to the surface," said Ryan, "that's going to be a big job, isn't it?"

The Doctor grinned. "Not with the TARDIS."

"I can't wait to see that big old box again," said Ryan. "No offence, Ash, but I'm not suited to living underground."

"That's all right, Ryan," she said. "How you people can bear to live up here, with nothing between you and the vast and empty void, I don't understand either."

Ryan's eyes widened. He hadn't thought of that before.

The Doctor laughed. "Poor Ryan. Hit with existential dread, and he hasn't even had his fry-up. All right, you two – I think I've got past the security protocols, should be able to shut down the drills completely." She linked her hands together and flexed the fingers. "Here goes nothing."

She thumped some buttons. Nothing immediately happened.

"Is that it?" said Ryan. "Brilliant!"

An alarm sounded, shrill and angry. Red lights started flashing, and then klaxons went off. A voice boomed through the base: *Intruders! Intruders!*

"Oops," said the Doctor. She bent over the controls on the console again.

"What's happening?" said Ash. "What's going on?"

The Doctor's hands were flying over the controls. "Must be a secondary security system, launching coun-termeasures." She looked up, her face bleak. "Satellites, in orbit, firing down on the surface."

Suddenly, the building shook around them. Ash looked scared. "What's happening?"

"High up above the surface, there are machines with weapons," said the Doctor. "They can fire at us, from up there. When I switched off the drills, something alerted those machines. So they've started attacking us."

"But why?" Ash said. "Why would anyone do that?"

"Protecting their investment!" said Ryan. "Doctor, I don't want to hang around here and get blown up. Can't we get back down underground?"

The Doctor's face was bleak. "No, Ryan. We won't be safe. All this will finish off what the drilling was doing – and quicker."

"The fissure," said Ash.

The ground beneath them shuddered again.

"It's being bombed from above," said Ryan. "Doctor, how do we stop it?"

She didn't answer.

After the Doctor's avatar disappeared, Emerald turned furiously on Quartz. "Are you happy now?" she said. "There'll be panic, chaos, riots! People are going to get hurt!"

"I don't think so," said Graham. "I think people are getting ready to help."

"Of course," said Yaz. "The Great Family. You all pull together."

"That's right," said Quartz. He began to head towards the door. "You underestimate us, Emerald. We can help Basalt to stop this."

Emerald, watching him leave, turned to the Greenwatch, standing by. "Stop him!" she ordered them. The group of guards looked at each other, anxiously. One or two took a step forwards but, seeing that they weren't in the majority, they held back, and went no closer to Quartz.

"I ordered you to stop him!" Emerald said.

Onyx moved forwards. "Emerald," he said, "they won't take your orders. Not over this." He turned to the others. "I suggest you help Quartz," he said. "That's what I'll be doing. It's long past time that we pulled together."

There were a few mutters amongst the Greenwatch. One or two remained where they were, but the majority headed for the door and left. Onyx and Quartz were about to follow, when the Doctor's avatar appeared again. Her expression was grim.

"Doctor," said Yaz. "What's the matter? Haven't you been able to stop the drilling?"

"Oh, we've stopped it all right. But turning off the drilling has turned on an automatic security system. We're being fired on from orbit. You won't be able to feel it all the way down there, but the bombardment could cause as much damage as the drilling. If not more. And faster."

Emerald, who had been listening to all of this, gave a bitter laugh. "I told you not to interfere!"

"The question is," said the Doctor coolly, "what are you going to do to help, Emerald? Everyone here tells me what a good leader you've been over the years, looking after your people when trouble came, making sure they were safe. Thing is, I've not seen anything to show me that you care about anything other than being proved right. And that's not leadership. That's betrayal."

Yaz, who was watching Emerald closely, saw how hard that struck.

"So," the Doctor went on, "things are going from bad to worse." Her image crackled with static and she staggered, as if rocked by an earth tremor. "What are you going to do,

Emerald? Let the damage get past the point of no return, just to prove yourself right? Or help to save your people?"

"You had *no* right to interfere!" said Emerald.

"I don't like to stand by and watch people kill themselves and take others with them," said the Doctor. "It's a fault I have, I know—"

"Doctor," Graham murmured. "This might not be helping."

"I need my TARDIS, Emerald," said the Doctor. "My blue box. I can save you all, if I have my TARDIS."

"Onyx knows where it is," said Graham. "I'll find him—"

"I had it moved," Emerald said, quickly. "You won't find it."

Graham threw his hands up in frustration.

"How long do we have, Doctor?" said Yaz.

"I don't know." The image of the Doctor broke up as she was almost thrown flat on her face. "An hour or so, maybe, before the fissure starts to crack beyond repair."

"What happens then?" said Graham.

"Then?" The Doctor sighed. "Then the seawater will start to flood through, and it will hit the hot lava, and that whole beautiful place where you're standing right now will be filled with steaming water, one huge steaming pool! Go and look out of the window, Emerald. Take a look at the people down there – the people you've been trying to help! Your inaction is harming them, more and more all the time!"

Then one of her Greenwatch stepped forwards. "We trusted you, Emerald. We've done everything you asked! And now we're asking you – help her!"

"At *last*," murmured the Doctor.

Emerald's expression crumbled. "All right, all right!" she cried. She turned to the watchmen. "I had the blue box taken to the fourth hall, where no one could see it." She looked down at the ground. "Have it brought here."

"No need," said the Doctor. "Yaz and Graham can get it."

"Doctor," said Graham, "we can't fly that thing!"

"Graham," she said, "I'll be standing right next to you. Well, this avatar will. I can talk you through it. Now go on – go and get that gorgeous ship of mine."

"What do we do when we get there?" said Yaz.

"Pack her high," she said. "Whatever Basalt needs. Then I'll talk you through flying her up to him. And then you can bring her up to me. Oh, I've missed her!"

One of the watchmen was waiting to lead the way. But the Doctor had one more thing to say. "Emerald. You're doing the right thing. I know you've been alone, trying to do all this by yourself – but you're not alone now. You wanted help. This is help. That's what I am, that's what I do. I help." The image wobbled alarmingly, dissolving into static. "Now – Yaz, Graham, get your skates on!"

"A *job*?" Ryan looked at the Doctor. "A *good* job?"

The Doctor took him by the arm to steady him as the room lurched under the impact of another missile close by – he supposed the security systems wouldn't target the control area and destroy the company's assets, they'd be blanket bombing to get any intruder transport in the area – and started leading him over to one of the consoles. "I promise you, Ryan, you're gonna love this."

Next thing Ryan knew, he'd been plonked unceremoniously into one of the chairs. The Doctor was reaching for some kind of headset. Ryan looked at it suspiciously. It had lots of wires coming out, and – was he imagining it, or were some of them wiggling about under their own power?

"Doctor, you're not planning on putting that thing on my head, are you?"

She was, and she did.

"This won't hurt," said the Doctor.

"Ow!"

"Oh, all right, it might hurt. Sorry."

"Something jabbed me, Doctor. My head! Jabbed!"

"Shush. Here, put your hand on these controls."

She shoved two long levers towards him and he grabbed hold of them.

"Now," she said. "Wait a second, I've just got to press some buttons…"

"Oh, great, that always works out well."

Ryan heard, rather than saw, her press some buttons. They jangled cheerfully. Then everything went dark, and, suddenly, he was looking out across a vast starscape at dozens upon dozens of small satellites. "Oh my days," said Ryan.

"*That's* what's firing at us."

"They can't hurt me, can they?" said Ryan.

"No, they can't," said the Doctor. "Well, yeah, they can if they hit us down here, or if the ground collapses beneath us, or whatever, but that's what you're there for. Start firing back!"

"What?"

"You're controlling one of the satellites, Ryan. You're operating the systems up there. I've checked for life signs. They're not manned. So start firing!"

"Are you sure this'll work, Doctor?"

"Nope. But it's our best plan. So go for it! While I try to fly the TARDIS by remote control…"

He went for it. And within seconds he realised that it was brilliant; like being completely immersed in one of his favourite games. But with a console you always felt as if you were taking part at a distance. Not with this. This was as good as being there. And then – *boom!* He was knocked out of the system. He raised the headset, and shook his head clear.

Ash came running over to him. "Are you all right? What happened?"

"I'm fine," Ryan said. "But I think they're smart. I think they learn. I think they worked out which satellite I was firing from."

"Try another satellite?" the Doctor said.

"They'll work that out too," he said. "I reckon I can do better than that. I think I can move around."

She grinned at him. "I knew you were the man for this job."

He put the headset back on. He was right. Shifting around from satellite to satellite kept him from being thrown out. After he'd taken out ten or fifteen of the other satellites, he realised he was humming the *Star Wars* theme. "Poe Dameron's got nothing on me," he said, as he blew another target out of the sky.

Again, the building shook. "Come on, Ash," said the Doctor, hurrying her towards a chair. "There's another headset here…" Soon Ash was firing at satellites too. The Doctor went over to another console to talk to Yaz and Graham. "Oh, this is frustrating," she said. "If I could just get my hands on those controls…"

"Woah!" said Ryan. "Out again!"

"All right, Yaz, Graham, listen. I'm going to show you how to set the coordinates… I hope…"

Suddenly, a crackle of static sounded through the control centre. Ryan pulled off the headset. "What was that?"

"I think someone's trying to talk to us…" The Doctor looked up and around. "Who's there?"

The static crackled again, and then a voice came through. *"Hello? Hello? Is there anyone there?"*

"Yeah," said the Doctor. "Me. I'm here. The Doctor. Who are you?"

"I'm… I'm a representative of the Actilliasauraitius Mining Corporation."

"Oh," said the Doctor. "That sounds very important. All right, representative – any way we could talk in person?"

There was a pause, and then: *"That won't be possible!"*

"Aw, come on!" said the Doctor. "I want a word with you – let's do it face to face!"

Eleven

There was a weird *whooshing* noise, and the space in front of Ryan and the Doctor shimmered. Slowly, a shape appeared – a short, stocky figure, humanoid, wearing some kind of protective spacesuit, and holding a device aloft in a hand that had a plenitude of fingers. Ryan remembered what Basalt had said about the bodies they had found. This was surely one of the same species.

"Doctor," whispered Ryan, "this isn't a hologram, is it?"

"No," said the Doctor. "This is the real deal." She waved at the arrival. "Hiya! No need for the protective suit, no gas to worry about now." She took a deep breath in and out, then frowned. "Just a lot of other stuff."

"Ah," said the figure. "I didn't really expect the transport link would still be working."

"But it is. *Everything's* still working, that's the trouble. Come on, let's speak face to face."

Slowly, the new arrival complied. It took a minute or two, but then it was standing there. It had beautiful pearlescent skin, smooth and hairless, and a face like a full moon. This was all slightly offset by the fact that it was wearing what looked like a very grubby T-shirt. The device it was holding was now plainly a cup, clutched very tightly in one hand.

"So," said the Doctor. "Who do we have here?"

"I told you," it said. "I'm a representative of the, um, the Actilliasauraitius Mining Corporation."

"You don't sound very sure about that," said the Doctor.

"I don't believe that's a real word," said Ryan. "Actilly... Nah. Not buying it."

"Yes it is! And I am!" Its voice was shaking, which slightly undercut the confidence with which it was trying to speak. "And I'd like to know what you're doing messing around with our security systems!"

"Are you all right?" The Doctor nodded at the cup. "Is that caffeine? Too much of that's bad for you, you know. Makes you jittery, gives you the shakes."

"Stop talking!" it said. "Explain yourselves!"

The Doctor looked round, then patted her chest. "Oh, you were talking to me! Oh no, no, I don't explain myself! Not very often. And not very well either. But I think *you* have some explaining to do."

A sheen was gathering over the pearly skin. "What do you mean?"

"I mean," said the Doctor, "that your mining corporation has almost caused a planetary cataclysm here! Digging too deep, tunnelling away without due care and attention! There are people here, you know – a whole sentient species of quiet, self-contained people, just getting on with their business and not causing any trouble—"

It stared back at her. "Another *species*? There wasn't anything about that on the files—"

"Yes, well, there is," said the Doctor, an edge coming into her voice, "and they're a quiet and peaceful people, who mean no harm to anyone—"

From over at the other console, absorbed in her new and alien virtual world, Ash yelled, "Gotcha!"

"*Most* of the time, anyway," said the Doctor.

The alien was goggling at Ash. "Is that... a *rock*?"

Ryan leaned in to have a quiet word. "Doctor," he said softly, "do you get the feeling that we're talking to the intern?"

"I mean," it said, "a living *rock*? We mine rocks, we don't expect them to have a hearbeat!"

The Doctor nodded. "There is something funny going on, isn't there?" She turned back to it. "Is your boss around?"

"My boss? Er, no! No!"

"Are you in trouble?" said the Doctor.

The sheen was covering its skin again. "Look, I'm only in my second week. I'm not meant to respond to these kind of calls and I'm not supposed to use the transporter and I'm certainly not meant to pass myself off as management. But all these alarms went off and I thought, 'Did I press the wrong button?'"

"Easily done," said the Doctor. "If you're not as good at buttons as I am."

"Is it true?" the alien said. "About a cataclysm and a whole sentient species under threat?" It looked at Ash. "Like *that*?"

"Like *her*," said the Doctor, "but, yeah. They live under the surface and the drilling is destroying their world. Will you help? Make it stop?"

It goggled at her. "I don't know if I can..."

"I know that you can," said the Doctor. "Hey, what's your name?"

"Me?" it said. "I'm Ouolulu."

"All right, Ouolulu," said the Doctor, "come here and show me what you can do."

Ouolulu joined her at the console and started operating controls. "I'm trying to see if there are any files about this planet. It's a while since anyone looked at this one... Oh, I see. Yes, there was a Stage 1A11 investigatory mission sent out, unpersonned, and that was followed up by Stage 1B12(a) landing party and preliminary dig. And then everything got cancelled... I wonder why..."

"It didn't get cancelled," said the Doctor. "That's the whole problem! The drilling carried on—"

"Still drilling?" said Ouolulu. "No, that's not right..."

The room shook harder than ever. "But it's happening. And a whole species is about to be destroyed!"

"Right, I'm with you. Hang on a moment... Ah!" said Ouolulu. "I see now! Oh.... Oh, no. Gas near one of the main shafts. Fatalities. Fourteen lost for good..."

Ryan looked at the Doctor. "We saw some of them."

"Our friends here found them," the Doctor said to Ouolulu. "They looked after the bodies. Now, can you help?"

"I can't switch off the security systems – I've not got anywhere near the authorisation."

Another *whoop* came from Ash's direction. "We're on top of that," said the Doctor. "Now, please—"

"I could give you the project files," Ouolulu said, doubtfully. "It would show you all the shafts, all the tunnels..."

"Keep talking," said the Doctor. "I'm interested."

"And you could put the nanobots into reverse instead of trying to shut them down, seal everything up. It's all here." Ouolulu showed her the files. The Doctor started scanning them. "You know, I should get back. I really shouldn't have been looking in these files..."

The Doctor looked up. "Ouolulu, you've solved a mystery. The families will be grateful."

Ouolulu went and got the protective suit, hit some buttons on it, and disappeared.

The Doctor shot Ryan a grin. "Come on, let's get Yaz and Graham here. And you, Ryan – get that headset on and back to work. There's still satellites firing at us – and Ash must have taken out far more than you by now!"

When the TARDIS was carried into Emerald's hall, Yaz was so glad to see it that she nearly ran up and threw her arms around her, like an old friend she hadn't seen in years. She ran her hands lovingly over the exterior. "Hey," she whispered. "I don't know if you can hear me, but it's nice to see you again."

Then Yaz sprang back in surprise as the doors swung abruptly open. Had she triggered some external mechanism, or...?

The Doctor's image appeared.

Graham jumped. "Stop doing that!" he said. "Man of my age – I could have a heart attack!"

"I'm quite shocked myself that the TARDIS opened up so easily." She grinned. "Mental command amplified by the crystal lattice. Impressive, don't you think?"

"Very, Doctor," said Yaz, nodding as she ran inside with Graham on her heels. "Now, what do we need to do?"

She listened as the Doctor issued instructions, and followed them obediently. "Will this work?" she said doubtfully. The Doctor's track record when it came to flying the TARDIS was… patchy at best.

"Enjoy it if it does," said the Doctor. "You know how fickle she can be. She'll appreciate the novelty but she won't make a habit of this."

The TARDIS juddered, and the console shifted into action.

"And we're off," said Graham. "I hope."

Yaz, concentrating on the Doctor's directions, ran her hands quickly over the controls to start the dematerialisation process. The TARDIS landed, softly.

"Don't tell the Doctor," said Graham, "but that was better than she's ever parked it."

"Graham," said the Doctor, "I'm standing right here. Well, not actually right here, but you know what I mean." She waved her hands at them. "Come on then, hurry up!"

Yaz poked her head out of the TARDIS door, and saw a shabby control room. There was the Doctor – for real, this time – and, sitting in two chairs alongside each other, were Ash and Ryan, wearing strange headgear and pulling at controls. Graham, stepping out of the TARDIS, took one look at his grandson and shook his head. "Don't tell me he found time to get a game in!"

"He's seeing off those satellites," said the Doctor. "Important and necessary work."

"*Yes!*" shouted Ryan, and punched the air. He lifted the headset and pulled it off. "That's the lot, Doctor," he said, and then saw his friends. "You made it! Shall we get going, then?"

Ash, who had also taken off her headset, came slowly towards the TARDIS. "Yes," she said, "this is what I saw, all those days ago, and I knew we weren't alone any longer. I knew someone had come to help us." She looked at the Doctor. "What's in there, Doctor?"

The Doctor held out her hand. "Wonderful things."

The TARDIS rematerialized on the platform near where the train had brought them. The friends stepped out, Ash with them. The Doctor placed her hand gently against the exterior of the old blue box. "Beautiful," she whispered.

They waited for Basalt to scramble over and join them. He stood in front of the TARDIS, palpably itching to touch the big old machine.

"Go on," said the Doctor. "But be gentle with her."

Basalt laid his hand on the TARDIS. "Alive!" he cried, and then started to laugh.

"Alive? In a way, yeah." The Doctor patted the TARDIS. "My oldest, bestest friend."

Basalt drew Ash into a hug. "My girl."

"Dad," she said, her eyes shining. "Out there. The surface. You won't believe what it's like!"

He smiled at her. "You've been further than I ever have. You, Ash! The furthest any of us has ever been!" He turned back to the Doctor. "So what happened?"

"I spoke to the, er, the people who did all this. They had no idea that you were here."

"Doctor," said Yaz, "there's so much damage… How do we even begin to fix this?"

"Do we have enough time?" said Ryan. "Before the fissure cracks wide open?"

"There's always a way," said the Doctor. "What do we have now that we didn't have before?"

Yaz thought for a while. "The nanobots!"

"The nanobots," said the Doctor. "And with what I learned from our friend, I can re-programme them, set the process into reverse, seal up the shafts, and the tunnels, and we're done. All Basalt and his people need to do is hop aboard the TARDIS here, and we can take them back home—"

"Leave?" said Basalt, and frowned. "Doctor, we can't leave. We're the only thing holding the fissure shut! If we leave – it cracks! Cracks wide!"

Yaz looked at the Doctor, and was surprised to see that, for once, she was completely wrong-footed. "Of course. The fissure wasn't made directly by the machines, it's a fault-line that's opened up – so the nanobots won't know to reverse it. I hadn't thought of that…"

"We'll stay," said Basalt, quickly. "You do what you need to do, and we'll stay and hold the fissure shut."

"Basalt," said the Doctor. "You don't understand. Everything will seal. You won't survive—"

"Will it help save people?" said Basalt.

"Dad…" said Ash, uncertainly.

Yaz looked at the Doctor. She couldn't put a name to this face: there were so many emotions passing over it. At last, the Doctor settled on determination. "No," she said. "No, I'm not having it. There's got to be another way."

"I can't see what else we can do," said Basalt. "And the longer we leave these shafts open, the worse the strain on the fissure gets. Doctor, do what you need to do!"

"What needs to be done," said the Doctor, "is that we start thinking."

Ash took his hand. "Dad," she said. "I believe in you. I know you'll come up with something."

But Basalt was shaking his head. "It's no use, Ash," he said. "Sometimes, you have to know when you're beaten."

In the Diamond City, people were watching and waiting, fearfully. Quartz was out and about, booming cheerfully in his big voice, keeping morale high. Onyx was out too, wearing his green stone, making sure the Greenwatch kept the peace and stopped any panic. And then – in all the shining halls and glittering walkways of the City, the Doctor appeared, larger than life, and with a beaming smile.

"Hello!" she said. "Me again. I'm here with Basalt. He wants a word."

The Doctor's avatar disappeared, and Basalt appeared instead. "Can they really see me?"

"We can see you, Basalt," said Quartz, dryly.

"Ah, good. Well, it's good to speak to you again, Quartz. I need you to do something for me. I need something from my study."

Quartz looked at him in horror. "Basalt, it's gone."

"Gone?"

Onyx stepped forwards. "Not all of it. Basalt – what do you need?"

"There were notes on crystal formations... What do you mean my study is gone?"

"Emerald had it destroyed," said Quartz.

"I saved what I could," said Onyx. "Let's hope I saved what we needed. Basalt, tell me what you want."

Up by the fissure, Basalt put his head in his hands. "My life's work," he said. "All gone."

"No, not all of it!" cried Yaz. "The cellar – we hid some there, and Onyx took most of your library and a pile of notes with him."

"But the study... The samples..."

Graham looked at him sadly. "We did what we could."

Faintly, they heard one of the crystal communicators hum. It was Quartz. *"I think we've found what you need..."*

Yaz watched as the Doctor and Basalt sat, hunched over and heads together, hard at work. She turned to Ryan. "I wonder what they'll come up with."

"Something weird. Something wonderful." He looked over his shoulder, back towards the fissure. There was a shout from up there, and one of the rock-people came dashing out. Water was trickling down the ground behind them. Ryan sighed. "I just hope they hurry."

The Doctor jumped suddenly to her feet. "All right," she said. "I think I know what we need to do, but we need to speak to Ouolulu again." She dashed towards the TARDIS. Yaz and Ryan chased after her.

The Doctor opened a communications channel. "Ouolulu. Ouolulu! It's me, the Doctor, back at the mine! We need your help!"

There was a short pause, and no response.

"Ouolulu! Are you there?"

Again, another silence, and then the alien's voice came through the comm. *"Hello? I'd just gone to get a snack. What do you need? I'm going off shift in a minute or two, got to figure out how I report this—"*

"I need the technical specifications for the nanobot technology you used here."

There was a soft laugh at the other end of the comm. *"On its way, Doctor."*

"Why the laughing?" said Ryan.

"Yeah, good point," said the Doctor. "Hey, why are you laughing?"

"Proprietary technology, Doctor! Anything else you'd like while I'm here?"

"You're doing the right thing," the Doctor said, helpfully.

"Sure. Will you write me a reference for my next employers?"

"If we make it," the Doctor said. She cut the comm channel, then starting reading through the information Ouolulu had sent. "Yes," she said, "I think I can see what to do…"

"Go on," said Yaz. "Tell us!"

"Basalt has detailed notes on the composition of the crystals up near the fissure, and he's done experiments on super-heating them. We thought for a while we could use that to weld it shut, but the process is too slow, and then I thought…" She smiled at Yaz. "Well, you know already."

Yaz smiled. "The nanobots?"

"That's right," said the Doctor. "I've had a look through the specs now, and I think I can programme them to interface with the crystals up by the fissure, so that when we send them into reverse, they'll close the natural holes as well as the artificial ones. Well, that's the theory."

"Will it work, Doctor?" said Ryan.

The Doctor pulled a face. "It should. It might. Perhaps. We'll need to get away quickly, though. If the fissure starts to crack and we're still here, we'll be first to go."

"And if it doesn't work, Doctor?" Yaz said softly. "What do we do then?"

The Doctor looked grim. "Then we go back to the Diamond City and we fill the TARDIS with everyone who'll come, and we get them away from here."

Yaz thought about the wonderful people she had seen. How would they live, away from this precious world of theirs? Where else could they possibly go?

"Come on," said the Doctor. "It's time to get started."

They headed for the TARDIS doors, stopping when Graham put his head round. He looked grim. "There you are," he said. "You'd better hurry. I don't think it's going to be much longer here."

They dashed back out onto the platform. Yaz looked round in horror. The trickle of water had become a free-flowing stream, and it was getting stronger by the second. Basalt was in the thick of it, organising his people to block up the crack, but it was clear they were fighting a losing battle.

"You three," said the Doctor, "get inside. Now!"

They did as she'd ordered, but Yaz stood by the doors and watched as the Doctor dashed towards Basalt. "Basalt!"

she cried. "We've got to go! Get your people away from there and into the TARDIS."

Yaz saw Basalt hesitate. "He doesn't want to leave," she murmured. "He knows that they're the only thing stopping the flood..."

"He'd better leave," said Graham. "Or he'll take us with him."

They stood back from the doors as Basalt's people dashed inside, taking cover in the TARDIS. Ash was last, and she stood at the door with Yaz, watching fearfully at her father, still hesitating. "Dad!" she cried. "You've got to come now!"

Basalt, hearing her cry, turned, and smiled at her. For a moment, Yaz was sure he was saying goodbye, and then he turned to the Doctor, and nodded, and, with her, ran towards the TARDIS. Behind them, the water was gushing freely now, and they skidded on the wet surface as they made for the TARDIS doors. Yaz and Ash jumped out of the way to let Basalt enter, and, last of all, the seawater lapping at her heels, the Doctor dashed inside, sealing the TARDIS doors behind her.

She ran towards the console, gabbling as she pushed and pulled the controls to make the TARDIS dematerialise. "I know, I know – bigger on the inside, dead exciting, all of time and space, I'll run you through the rest later. Right now – got some nanobots to hack. Wish me luck!"

Yaz felt Ryan move to stand next to her, and was relieved to have her friend by her side once again. Graham stood behind them, like a mother hen watching over chicks. Yaz saw Ash take her father's hand. She watched as the water flooded through onto the platform, and she gasped as the roof of the tunnel began to buckle and collapse.

And then the Doctor cried, "Here we go—!"

Down in the City, the people of looked up at the roof of the world. As they watched, a white light spread across the heavens.

Silence fell.

And then there was a strange, unearthly grinding noise. Someone screamed, which set a few others off. Someone else cried out, "It's happening! We're all going to die!"

Inside the TARDIS, everything was very still. "Doctor," said Ryan, uncertainly. "Did that work?"

The Doctor was taking readings at the console. "Surface shaft, closing," she muttered. "Tunnel, closing. Secondary shaft, closing…"

"What about the fissure?" said Basalt.

"Wait for it, wait for it…" The Doctor was concentrating on the controls like Ryan had never seen her do before. "Come on, come *on*…"

The Diamond City was teetering on the edge of panic. "We're finished!" someone cried, and some people began to look around, for somewhere to escape… But others were still looking upwards. Pointing upwards, they cried, "No, look! The threads of light – they're gone! The cracks are closing!"

And someone else said, "Where did that blue box come from?"

The Doctor looked up at Basalt and smiled. "Sealed," she said. "The fissure's sealed for good."

Ash put her arm around her father. "You did it," she said. "You saved us."

He shook his head. "*She* saved us. Thank you, Doctor. I wish I knew what you'd done!"

She beamed at him. "I'll run you through it. These nanobots – you're going to love them."

"Proprietary technology, Doctor?" said Yaz, with a smile.

"Compensation," said the Doctor, firmly. "Now – one last job." She looked down at the console again.

"What are you doing?" said Ryan.

"Just a little hack into the files of a certain mining corporation," she said. "Not something I do every day of the week, but I think it's easier this way. Off the record, as it were. Put a marker round this world – don't come near." She smiled at Basalt and Ash. "You don't want any more visitors poking about your home for commercial gain. Although you might consider doing some visiting to other worlds one day." She went back to the console. "Oh, and I've recommended our friend back there a full-time job. I think Ouolulu earned it."

One-by-one, they came out of the TARDIS. The people of the Diamond City were not slow in showing their appreciation. The noise of their applause was a booming cacophony, rock on rock, stones singing.

"This is more like it," said Graham. "Better than getting chucked into a dungeon."

Last of all, Basalt came out of the TARDIS, and the people of the City roared his name. He stood blinking at them, overcome with emotion.

"Hero of the hour," said the Doctor. "Good."

Ash was beaming with pleasure. "This is all I ever wanted," she said. "I wanted everyone to know that he was right."

"Don't forget everything you did, Ash," Ryan said. "You've gone further than anyone on your world ever has before."

Ash smiled. "So I did," she said.

Yaz nudged the Doctor. "Look," she said. "Emerald."

They watched as, slowly, Emerald also began to applaud. The Doctor slipped over to speak to her.

"I suppose," said Emerald, lowering her hands, "that I should say thank you."

"That's all right," said the Doctor. "I wish you'd listened sooner, that's all. What will you do?"

Emerald sighed. "I believe... that from now on, I shall leave things in Quartz's hands."

"I kind of thought that might happen. But what are *you* going to do?"

Emerald turned to look straight at the Doctor. "I want to learn," she said. "Learn from Basalt."

The Doctor beamed at her. "That sounds about right," she said. "Help him rebuild that study. Make it bigger and better than ever before. Build a school. Build a *university*. Who knows what you're starting here?" She put her hand on Emerald's glittering shoulder. "This is where you turn things around. Make the fear and the chaos your people have lived through worth it."

The Doctor and her friends stayed for a little while longer to celebrate, before saying goodbye to new friends and leaving this world for another adventure. But there was one more quick journey to make first, and for Yaz it was the best part of the whole experience.

The TARDIS landed again up on the surface. No, this wasn't a remarkable world, all told – at least, not up here. Yaz could see moors like this back at home, in Yorkshire, and they'd be better there, because they were Yorkshire moors. But what she couldn't see back home was Basalt, standing at last for a brief time on the surface of his world, face turned up and out to see the huge sky, the vast heavens, and the whole universe – as he had always imagined it would be.